GENERATION
S.L.U.T.

(SEXUALLY LIBERATED URBAN TEENS)

A Brutal Feel-Up Session with Today's Sex-Crazed Adolescent Populace

Marty Beckerman

POCKET BOOKS   **bOOKS**

New York • London • Toronto • Sydney

GENERATION S.L.U.T.

An Original Publication of MTV Books/Pocket Books

POCKET BOOKS, a division of Simon & Schuster, Inc. 1230 Avenue of the Americas, New York, NY 10020

MTV Music Television and all related titles, logos, and characters are trademarks of MTV Networks, a division of Viacom International Inc.

ISBN: 0-7434-7109-1

First MTV Books/Pocket Books trade paperback printing February 2004

10 9 8 7 6 5 4 3 2

POCKET and colophon are registered trademarks of Simon & Schuster, Inc.

Cover Design Direction: Deklah Polansky

Cover Design & Photography: Alison Roberto

Grateful acknowledgment is made to Brett Gurewitz (Bad Religion) for use of the lyrics to "Sanity," "21st Century Digital Boy" and Jesse Michaels (Operation Ivy) for use of lyrics to "Knowledge."

Manufactured in the United States of America

For information regarding special discounts for bulk purchases, please contact: Simon & Schuster Special Sales at 1-800-456-6798 or business@simonandschuster.com

DESIGN + ART: theBRM

GENERATION S.L.U.T.

"Original. Hilarious. Well crafted and outrageous, yet with a moral compass that never quits. Parents will be shocked senseless by what they find here, but for younger readers, Marty Beckerman emerges as—dare I say it—a voice for a new generation."
—Richard Metzger, Author, Book of Lies: The Disinformation Guide to Magick and the Occult

"A thing of beauty. Beckerman exposes pedophile culture in a way that everyone else is afraid to do. Generation S.L.U.T. is something special."
—Ned Vizzini, Author, Teen Angst? Naaah . . . and Be More Chill

"The quality of Beckerman's writing is astonishing. Generation S.L.U.T. achieves a glorious momentum that compels the reader to keep turning the pages—and eagerly so. A wonderful window into the lives of young people today."
—Rodger Streitmatter, Ph.D., Author, Mightier Than the Sword: How the News Media Have Shaped American History

"Beckerman's angry, vulgar, smart voice is both tempered and amplified by an almost philosophical understanding of his situation. I read this and think of Lenny Bruce, and there's little praise higher."
—Carrie Hill Wilner, Nerve.com

"This kind of insight usually comes only with advanced age. Imagine going through your hormone-crazed teenage sexual peak with full self-awareness and an uncanny knack for cutting through pretenses and reporting the brutal truth. Just the right mix of shocking, tragic, and hilarious. The work of a 20-year-old genius. I'm giving one to every slut I know."
—Jenna Glatzer, Editor in Chief, AbsoluteWrite.com

"Generation S.L.U.T. firmly establishes Marty Beckerman as the Lenny Bruce of his generation. The best and funniest book about young lust I've read in ages, yet also sweet and romantic in ways that will get him laid a lot."
—John Strausbaugh, Author, Rock Til You Drop: The Decline from Rebellion to Nostalgia

"The blackest satire I've seen in some time. This could be quite controversial, especially if and when it gets banned. The sick thing—the reason I see a big fuss being made about it—is there are a lot of fundamental truths of modern teen existence in there."
—Todd Allen, Indignant Online

"An assault on the mind and soul. Sexual but not sexy, violent but never unrealistic. An impressive, ambitious debut that should be read by every teen and parent."
—Bob Sassone, Professor Barnhardt's Journal

This book is dedicated, with overflowing sympathy,
to every eighteen-year-old virgin on Planet Earth.

Thank Christ I wasn't one of you poor fuckers for long.

Special thanks:

Jim Fitzgerald
Jacob Hoye
John Strausbaugh
Ned Vizzini
Rodger Streitmatter
Bob Sassone
Jessica Mauer
Mom and Dad
Snoopy the Wonder Dog

AUTHOR'S NOTE ON STATISTICS:

ANYONE CAN MAKE ANY PUBLIC STUDY SAY NEARLY ANYTHING. THE STATISTICS HEREIN ORIGINATE FROM THE MOST RECENT AND REPUTABLE NATIONAL STUDIES AVAILABLE, BUT THE NUMBERS CHANGE FROM DAY TO DAY AND ONLY REPRESENT SPECIFIC SURVEY POOLS. SUBSEQUENTLY, THESE STATISTICS SHOULD NOT BE TAKEN AS AN ABSOLUTE REFLECTION OF REALITY, BUT INSTEAD THE MOST METICULOUS REPRESEN-TATION POSSIBLE AT THIS TIME.

O shame, where is thy blush?
Rebellious Hell...
To flaming youth let virtue be as wax
And melt in her own fire. Proclaim no shame
When the compulsive ardor gives the charge,
Since frost itself as actively doth burn.
—SHAKESPEARE

Has not Nature proved, in giving us the strength to submit to our
desires, that we have the right to do so?
—MARQUIS DE SADE

Poet, by that God to you unknown, lead me this way . . .
and be my guide through the sad halls of hell.
—DANTE

"'Hooking Up' was a term known in the year 2000 to almost every American child over the age of nine, but to only a relatively small percentage of their parents, who, even if they heard it, thought it was used in the old sense of "meeting" someone.... Back in the twentieth century, American girls had used baseball terminology. 'First base' referred to embracing and kissing; 'second base' referred to groping and fondling; 'third base' referred to fellatio, usually known in polite conversation by the ambiguous term 'oral sex'; and 'home plate' meant conception-mode intercourse, known familiarly as 'going all the way.' In the year 2000, in the era of hooking up, 'first base' meant deep kissing, groping and fondling; 'second base' meant oral sex; 'third base' meant going all the way; and 'home plate' meant learning each other's names."

—HOOKING UP BY TOM WOLFE, PICADOR USA, 2001

"Elizabeth Walters, a nurse midwife and counselor at the Health Interested Teens Own Program on Sexuality (HiTOPS) clinic in Princeton, recalls the recent visit of a mother and her 12-year-old son. 'He was this soccer-jock type,' she says. The mother had noticed that her son was withdrawn and irritable after sleep-away camp. 'The mom kept asking questions,' says Walters. Finally, as she was ferrying him from practice in the family minivan, he told her what was wrong: He had engaged in anal sex with a girl at camp. 'It was all she could do to keep the car on the road,' says Walters."

—U.S. NEWS & WORLD REPORT, MAY 27, 2002

S.L.U.T. STAT

Percentage of nonvirgin American 18-year-old boys: **80**
Percentage of nonvirgin American 18-year-old girls: **77**
Number of American teenagers who lose their virginity per day: **7,700**
[Source: The Alan Guttmacher Institute]

LISA C., 16

FARGO, NORTH DAKOTA

"Let's see, how many boys have I had sex with? Probably like three . . . eight . . . eleven . . . twelve . . . Yeah, probably like fourteen. Oh God. Hold on, I'm going to count on my fingers. Jerry, um . . . Mike, Casey, Aaron . . . Yeah, probably like fourteen."

S.L.U.T. STAT

Percentage of 15- to 17-year-old boys who feel pressure from friends to have sex: **67**
Percentage of 15- to 17-year-old girls who feel pressure from boys to have sex: **89**
Percentage of 15- to 17-year-old girls who believe it's acceptable for boys to have multiple sexual partners: **42**
Percentage of 15- to 17-year-olds who believe it's "bad" for a boy to be a virgin: **19**
[Source: The Kaiser Family Foundation/*Seventeen* Magazine, December 2002]

AMANDA, 13

SACRAMENTO, CALIFORNIA

[Quoted from *Middle School Confessions*, HBO Networks]

"I think we're just more of a generation that sex is being introduced to us at a younger age and that's why we're, like, eager to start it. . . . You know, my mom wasn't really into the whole sex scene when she was thirteen years old. And we are."

"Girls are as conversant today about condoms as they are about shoes and belly-button piercings, and proud of their expertise. 'I've carried one since I was 12,' says Amanda, a petite, soft-spoken girl who is on the track team. 'Lipstick and a condom, that's about all you need. You can't trust boys.' She hasn't actually had intercourse yet, but, she says, 'You never know.' At 16, she's given blowjobs to five boys. 'It was OK, no big deal. A little boring sometimes, because the guys don't say much, and you have to keep sucking until your mouth hurts. I always pretend I'm [actress] Drew Barrymore when I do it.'"

—SALON.COM, DECEMBER 14, 2000

"That women tend to be choosier than men about their sexual partners is, of course, exactly what is predicted by evolutionary theory; but since romantic love does not appear to be a universal human experience, one would not expect love to be the basis of female choice everywhere."

—THE EVOLUTION OF HUMAN SEXUALITY BY DONALD SYMONS, OXFORD UNIVERSITY PRESS, 1979

FRIDAY

"I'm not being a bitch." Max stepped from Brett's mattress to the snow-covered windowsill. "Like my manhood has anything to do with jumping out your stupid window."

"Your *manhood*?" Brett laughed. "Excuse me, *which* one of us has never kissed a girl in his entire fucking life?"

"Big deal." Max leapt out the window and hit the frigid ground on his side.

"But *tonight* . . . " Brett followed Max out the window and landed smoothly. "Well, they don't call it a make-out party for nothing, Maxwell. You're getting a slice whether you like it or not."

"I won't even *know* anyone there." Max lifted himself to his feet and wiped off both pant legs. "How do you get a slice from a girl you've never *met* before?"

"Just find a girl sitting by herself, make her laugh, tell her she's special or pretty or something. You'll get to second base *at least,* I swear to fucking Christ."

"So that's like tonguing and booby touching and stuff? Or what?"

"Pretty much." Brett took a cigarette from his tin of Altoids Wintergreen Mints. "But don't cram your tongue all the way down her throat or anything stupid like that, okay? And keep your lips closed when you move in for the kill, or else you're just going to make her gag before the All-American Teenage Suckfest even *commences*. And if—*if*—you actually *do* wind up with a girl tonight, and I'm not guaranteeing anything with that dazzling nose zit of yours, do *not* tell her she's your first kiss, all right? That was cool, like, three years ago, but now it's this fucking *chore*, you know? Girls like guys with *experience* now. So you'll just need to fake it."

"Okay. Sure. I'm *experienced,* baby. Like that?"

"Good Lord." Brett smirked. "You're getting a *slice.*"

"Wouldn't it feel weird though?" Max asked, following Brett past the ice-laden road, balling his fists within his coat pockets to keep his fingers warm. "Like, not even *knowing* a girl and then going all the way with her?"

"It just doesn't *matter* with these fuckin' bitches, dude. It's totally irrelevant whether you're you or I'm me—well, it probably helps that I'm me—but the point is we're fucking guys and that's all these stupid girls care about at these things, you know? And if all else fails, I'll just tell some little ninth-grade whore that I'll fuck her at the next party if she fucks you at this one."

"Um, Brett, really, I'm not sure I'd want to sleep with a girl I didn't even know before we had sex or whatev—"

"Or what the hell, I'll just fuck her at this one too. Hey, would you ever be into double teaming a girl or anything? I mean, we'd have to see each other's dicks and everything, but just think about how fucking *hot* it would be if I got the mouth and you got the sloppy motherfuckin' *puss*—"

"Gross, Brett . . . So how far till we get to Ashley Iverson's house? It's getting really cold out here."

"Settle down, fucker. We've still got a few blocks to go."

"So somebody's moving into the apartment across from mine tomorrow." Max nearly tripped over a patch of snow in the road. "I don't know who they are yet, but I guess I'm pretty excited about it."

"Oh yeah? Well, fuck you, faggot."

"I'm not gay, Brett. You know that."

"Oh yeah? Well, fuck you, faggot."

"So what's it like?" Max asked after five minutes of silence. "I mean, having sex with a girl and everything?"

"It's . . . It's not like jerking off." Brett lit another cigarette. "It's more like . . . shit, I don't *know,* man. It's so fucking hard to *describe.* I guess it's kind of like a warm apple pie or something, but . . . well, no, that's bullshit. . . . It's just one of those things that's not like anything except itself, you know?"

Silence.

"Well, fuck it." Brett smiled. "You'll find out soon enough. Granted, it might take some intervention from our good friend Christ Almighty, but I'd give you two more hours of virginity, tops. Congratulations, Maxwell. You're going to be a real boy soon."

"Well, I . . . I guess so, maybe. It's just . . . I don't know. Shouldn't your first time be kind of special or something?"

"*Special?*" Brett laughed. "Good *Lord*, Max. What? I never told you about *my* first time?"

"No . . . I don't think so. Who was it? Quinn Kaysen?"

"Naaah, dude. Some *college* girl. You remember when I visited my brother at U of O last year? Well, he had a few of his frat brothers over one night taking shots of vodka, right? And they all thought it would be a funny idea to get me *laid*. So they started brainstorming up girls who'd just broken up with their boyfriends or fucked anything that moves anyway, and they called this one girl down—I think her name was like Kia or Sarah or something—and my brother introduced me as a freshman visiting from out of town. Granted, I was a *high school* freshman, but we got this dumb bitch too drunk to know the fuckin' difference. I swear to God, man, all I said to this dirty whore was 'Where are you from?' and 'What's your major?' and she asked if I wanted to go back to her dorm room and 'cuddle.' We did fuckin' everything, dude. And I mean fuckin' *everything.*"

"Wow . . . And you really don't feel bad about forgetting her name?"

"Please, Maxwell. It was fucking amazing. And I wasn't even *drunk.*"

"Um . . . Um, Brett?" Max followed Brett past the two dozen Kapkovian Pacific Secondary School students conversing and attempting to stand on both feet in Ashley Iverson's front yard. "I'm not sure I'm going to fit in here too well."

"What are you talking about?"

"I'm . . . Brett, I'm *scared.*"

"*Scared? Of what? People?*"

"They're all *big.*" Max froze in place. "And they don't know me and they don't like me and they're all wearing Pike & Crew and I'm not and I can't I can't I can't I can't I—"

"Would you *chill the fuck out?* We're here to have fun, not nervous fucking *breakdowns.*"

"I know I know I'm sorry Brett I know I know I *know.*"

"Listen, Max . . . I'm going to tell you a secret, okay? Would you pull yourself together if I tell you a secret? Okay, *I'm scared too*, all right? *Everyone* here is fucking scared."

"They are?" Max breathed softer. "*You* are?"

"It's just this *standard*, right? You wear Pike & Crew, you fuck around at parties, you wear these stupid shell necklaces and get your hair highlighted and go tanning three hours a week, and *then* you can be judged by who you really are as a person. You just have to sacrifice a little individuality to be seen as an individual with these people."

"Then why—?"

"Why *what*, Max?"

"Why do you do it?"

"Shit . . . *I* don't know, man. I guess in some morbid, fucked-up way I kind of enjoy it. Now listen, I've just told you something about these people they don't even know about themselves, all right? So let's go inside, have a few shots, have a good time and I promise you'll think it was stupid to ever be scared of these whores in the first place, okay?"

"Okay . . ." Max bit his lower lip. "Sorry about freaking out and everything. I guess that wasn't a very cool thing to do."

"Don't worry about it, dude." Brett slapped Max on the back. "I'll try not to tell everyone here how much of a fucking pussy you can be sometimes."

Ashley smiled, breath already redolent of Bailey's Irish Cream, Absolut vodka, Malibu coconut rum and Bacardi Breezers. "Let's go upstairs so nobody sees there's more to drink. And don't worry about taking off your shoes, it's just something else for people to trip over."

"This is Max, by the way." Brett followed Ashley up the hardwood staircase, carefully analyzing her miniskirt-clad posterior. "Max, this is Ashley. She's too good for you, so don't even think about it."

"Stop, Brett." She blushed. "It's nice to meet you, Max."

"You too," Max said. "You're pretty. And special. Or something."

"*Ohhhhhhhhhhhh,*" Ashley cooed, leading Max and Brett into her darkened bedroom and closing the door. "There's a shot glass over there on my dresser."

"There would be, you alcoholic bitch." Brett reached for the shot glass next to an unopened blue Trojan condom wrapper.[1] "Big plans for tonight?"

"None involving you." Ashley sat on the mattress. "At least not in the immediate future."

"That's unfortunate." Brett filled the shot glass and drank. "So your parents are in Europe or something?"

"Thailand, I think. You look uncomfortable, Max. Do you want to sit here on the bed with me?"

"Okay." Max took a seat on the mattress. "Thanks."

"*Whore,*" Brett fake-coughed into one hand. "*Slut.*"

"Oh, fuck you, Brett," Ashley said. "Shouldn't you be out stalking Quinn Kaysen?"

"We're just friends now." Brett handed the shot glass to Ashley. "You know that, Ash."

"Oh, really?" She filled the glass and drank. "So I guess it shouldn't bother you who's been putting the moves on her all night. Max, do you want any to drink?"

"Okay . . . Sure." He took the bottle from Ashley, then nervously filled the glass, swallowed, and fell to his knees coughing and wheezing.

"Fucking shameful." Brett sighed. "First shot in his life."

"I'm—*kak-kak*—I'm *sorry,*" Max gasped. "Oh—*kak*—oh God. It burns."

"All right, you pitiful fucker, I'm going downstairs. Ash? You coming?"

"Oh . . . I'll stay," Ashley said. "He'll do better with the lemonade anyway."

"Of course he will." Brett opened the bedroom door. "Happy humping, gorgeous."

"All you need is fuck, all you need is fuck, fuck, fuck is all you need," Brett hummed to the tune of the Beatles' "All You Need is Love" as he walked downstairs to the capacious family room. Hundreds of Kapkovian Pacific students drank cheap beer out of plastic cups, cracked inside jokes dating back to junior high and gyrated feverishly in couples on the hardwood floors. Many other couples lay atop those same floors, not dancing so much as publicly fornicating.

"—beer's not so bad—"

"—like shots more—"

"—acquired taste—"

"—acquired taste like *pussy*—"

"—ever do anal if—"

---

1 / "TROJAN-ENZ BRAND LATEX CONDOM LUBRICATED: If used properly, latex condom will help to reduce the risk of transmission of HIV infection and many other sexually transmitted diseases. Also highly effective against pregnancy."

"—with a condom or—"

"—kind of an asshole, but he had a nice truck so I let him fuck me—"

"—hot as hell, but she's *Christian*—"

"—couple nails and a cross, have your fuckin' *way* with her, motherfucker—"

"Yo, Brett fuckin' Hunter." The quarterback of the Kapkovian Pacific football team staggered forth from the sweltering throng and thrust an Olympian arm across Brett's shoulders. "How's your bro liking Oregon?"

"He's liking it. Don't ever touch me." Brett shrugged the quarterback off and walked farther into the adolescent pandemonium.

"Oh my God, *Brett Hunter!*" A girl with auburn highlights grabbed onto Brett's leather belt and thrust her pelvis against his in rhythm with the computer-generated music blaring throughout the house. "Oh my *God,* I can't believe I'm *dancing* with the track champion of the *entire school.*"

"What's your name?" He dry humped the girl in return, placing one hand on her lower hip and the other over her gym-toned, Maui-tanned glutei maximi. "Shit, you're a good dancer."

"Brett! Over here!" Quinn Kaysen leapt from the leather sofa across the room. "Oh God, I thought you weren't *coming.*"

"Hug for Daddy?" Brett asked, pushing the auburn-haired girl back into the crowd. "Please? I'll pay you."

"Flirt." Quinn threw her arms around Brett's shoulders. "Where have you *been* all night?"

"Had a little trouble sneaking out, that's all—I didn't want to drive the Camry over 'cause my parents might've heard the engine. So is Two-Shot Quinn drunk yet?"

"Not really." She smiled. "Okay, *mayyybe* . . . Oh my God, Brett, you won't *believe* who just invited me to—"

"Your perfume smells *incredible,* by the way. Is that CK We? Or P & C Conformity?"

"Listen, Brett, you won't *believe* who just invited me to winter prom."

"Invited . . . you . . . to . . . *Who?*"

"Trevor *Thompson.* Can you *believe* that?"

"You're joking." Brett gulped. "Ha! Ha!"

"Oh my *God,* Brett, have you *seen* his new BMW? It's like the most beautiful car I've ever *been* in. And he just got his own *apartment.* Did you *know* that? Who has their own apartment *junior year?* And he's *such* a good kisser."

"Quinn, you . . . you can't . . . Trevor Thompson is *dangerous,* okay? You don't *know* him like I know him."

"Fuck you, Brett. We're not going *out* anymore, remember? You can't tell me what I can and can't fucking *do* with my life. I'm *over* you—why can't you get over me?"

"Did I hear someone say BMW?" Trevor wrapped his arms around Quinn's waist and kissed her neck. "Sorry for leaving you all alone, beautiful. Hope you did okay without me."

"You're so sweet." She smiled. "Oh, Trevor, this is my friend Brett Hunter, from the track team. Brett, this is Trevor *Thompson.* My *date* for tomorrow night."

"My parents gave me a copy of the book for Christmas." Brett shook Trevor's hand with ample pressure. "Congratulations, Trevor. Really."

"Thanks a lot, Hunter." Trevor grinned. "Hope it made you pregnant with knowledge."

"Tell him about the *second* one," Quinn said. "He's writing a *second* one, Brett."

"Basically it's the follow-up to *Investing for Teenagers,*" Trevor said. "I'm calling it *I Made a Million Dollars Before Turning Eighteen and So Can You: How to Conquer the Stock Market AND High School.* Random House and HarperCollins are already bidding seven figures over it and I haven't even written seven *pages* yet."

"Well, that's fucking great, Trevor." Brett clenched his teeth. "Quinn, I'm going to check up on Max now. I'll talk to you later, okay?"

"There's a party at my place this Tuesday, Hunter," Trevor said. "Consider yourself invited."

"Wait, Brett," Quinn said. *"You* asked a girl to prom, right?"

"No . . ." Brett turned away. "Couldn't find a girl worth asking."

"Whoa . . . not bad at all." Max set the empty bottle of Jack Daniel's Lynchburg Lemonade beside the five others on the oak dresser. "Sorry for going through the whole carton and everything. I guess I was pretty thirsty."

"It's fine." Ashley laughed. "Most guys won't even *admit* they like girly drinks—only crappy beer because I guess their dicks aren't big enough or something, so they have to keep proving their manhood to each other."

"Yeah, I don't see why getting drunk should taste gross, except Brett always says girly drinks are like the worst thing in the world you can put in your mouth besides another man's genitalia."

"God . . . How do you even put *up* with him?"

"I don't know . . . He's my best friend."

"He doesn't *treat* you like much of a friend."

"Well, I guess he can be a real asshole sometimes, but he's a good guy deep down, you know? I mean, obviously I'm not the most popular kid at school or anything, but with him it doesn't matter if I don't play sports or go to dances or whatever, because he does all those things anyway and just because I don't, why should that stop us from being friends?"

Silence.

"So . . . um . . . What kind of music do you listen to?" Max asked. "I mean, if you listen to music and everything."

"Whatever's on the radio, I guess. . . . What about you?"

"The Beatles mostly. Simon and Garfunkel too sometimes."

"The *Beatles?*" Ashley laughed. "My *parents* listen to the Beatles."

"Really? That's awesome . . . I mean . . . um . . . how lame. Oh God."

"Listen, sweetie." She clasped her hands over Max's forearms. "Are we going to hook up tonight or what?"

"Oh . . ." Max looked away, fervently studying the posters of pop singers and teen idols adorning the walls. "Hey, alcohol doesn't make you hallucinate, does it?"

"No." Ashley slid her hands up to Max's shoulders. "It doesn't make you hallucinate." Her tongue commenced performing somersaults inside his mouth.

"Whoa!" Max gasped. "That feels *awesome!"*

She laughed and moved his hands under her shirt and bra.

"Sorry." He blushed, staring down at his erection. "I . . . I can't really turn it on and off or anything like that."

"I like it when I make guys hard." She pulled Max's shirt over his head and then removed her own. "Lick my breasts?"

"Okay!" He buried his face in Ashley's chest just as Brett opened the bedroom door.

"Fuck!" Brett screamed.

"Crap!" Max screamed.

"Jesus God!" Brett screamed.

"Crap!" Max screamed.

"Hi Brett," Ashley said calmly. "Need something? Or do you just want to watch this time?"

"Never mind." Brett slammed the door. "I'm going home. I'll leave the window open for you, tiger."

(Long, awkward silence.)

"Oh God." Max exhaled. "That was really embarrassing."

"It's my fault for not locking the door." Ashley walked across the bedroom and secured the handle, then unhooked her black Pike & Crew silk bra and returned to the bed wearing only a matching pair of black panties. "You still *want* to, don't you?"

"I . . . No, I . . . I *do,* I really do . . . It's just that I don't want this to be meaningless for both of us and I'd never really kissed a girl before five minutes ago and I'm kind of scared even though you're very pretty and very nice and not wearing very many clothes."

"You're sweet." She unzipped the fly of his pants and pulled down his red and blue Spider-Man boxer shorts, then reached for the unopened Trojan wrapper on the dresser. "Don't resist the things you want, okay?"

"Okay . . ." Max closed his eyes and leaned back against the pillow.

Ashley kissed her way down to his chest and stomach, then ran her tongue up and down the shaft of his penis, massaging his testicles with one hand and stroking him with the other. She opened the Trojan wrapper and gently rolled the latex condom over Max's penis, then slipped off her black panties and lay supine on the mattress.

"Fuck me?" she whispered.

And Max knew one thing:

This was not love.

"Fuck you, Trevor," Brett said to himself, breaking through the orgiastic throng of drunken teenagers on his way to the front door. "Fucking pretentious two-faced backstabbing son of a dirty syphilis-ridden prostit—"

"You're still *here?*" The auburn-haired girl who had earlier dry humped Brett in the family room stumbled across the hallway. The thin straps of her Pike & Crew halter top slipped down her arms. "Oh my *God*, Brett. You're still *here.*"

"No shit." He pushed past the girl and opened the front door.

"Wait!" She threw herself in front of the door. "Please, I . . . Oh God, I know you probably think I'm just saying this because I'm drunk or whatever, but you look *so cute* tonight and you're *such* a good dancer and I just want to—"

"Oh Christ," Brett sighed. "All right. Fine. Where?"

"What about here?" She led Brett into a darkened closet crowded with shoes, jackets, dusty board games and a broken vacuum cleaner. "Oh God, I've wanted you so bad ever since you won at state finals last year. You have *no idea* how many times I've thought about this actually happening."

"What's your name?" Brett unzipped his fly.

"Holly." She kneeled and pulled down his plaid Pike & Crew boxer shorts. "I'm on the cheerleading squad."

She flicked her tongue across the tip of his penis—releasing her saliva onto his shaft as lubricant—then licked and suckled for nearly seventeen minutes. "Are you going to come or what?"

"I don't know," Brett shrugged, eyes closed. "I guess I just wish you were Quinn right now."

"What?" She lifted her head from Brett's saliva-coated groin. *"What the fuck did you just say to me?"*

"Nothing." Brett pulled up his boxer shorts and zipped his pants, then shut the closet door behind him.

"Back so early?" Brett lay in his bed, an open Budweiser atop his chest and one hand down the front of his plaid boxer shorts. "That Ashley's a real humper, all right. Can't last five *minutes* with a slut like that."

"Shut up, Brett." Max pulled himself over the windowsill into the bedroom. "She didn't even remember my *name.*"

"Some girls just lay there and don't *do* anything, but Ashley . . . fuck, man, Ashley gets *into* that shit."

"It didn't *mean* anything." Max's chest quivered. "It didn't mean *anything.*"

"So?" Brett lifted his head from the pillow. "What's the problem?"

"I didn't even *know* her. . . . Oh God, I didn't . . . didn't even . . ."

"Fuck girls, man." Brett swigged the Budweiser. "Let me tell you something, all right? When I was fourteen my brother snuck me into this strip club downtown. And this girl who worked there—she couldn't have been a fuckin' day over eighteen—my brother starts giving her all these tips, you know? So after he burns twenty or thirty bucks, this bitch gives him a lap dance—rubs her tight stripper ass all over his crotch, shoves her gorgeous titties in his face, all that—and he keeps giving her more and more *money*, right? Pretty soon she asks if he wants to go into the back, but he just smiles and points at me. Before I know it, I'm pinned against a bathroom stall with this goddamn stripper's hands down my pants."

"Heartwarming, Brett." Max sniffled. "You really know how to cheer a guy up."

"You know what I told my brother later? *'I didn't even know her.'* Swear to God, Max, I was crying my fucking brains out just like you are now. And this is what my brother told me—'Brett, it happened. You can either hate yourself forever or just admit you loved every second of it.' Now come on, Max. Be honest for once in your life."

"Oh God . . ." Max covered his face with both hands. "It felt so good."

"Well, Christ, I *knew* that." Brett rolled facedown onto the pillow. "Night, fucker."

↗ S.L.U.T. STATS

Percentage of sexually active eighteen-year-olds in 1959: **23**
Percentage of sexually active eighteen-year-olds in 1968: **42**
Percentage of sexually active eighteen-year-olds in 1972: **55**
Percentage of sexually active eighteen-year-olds in 1982: **64**
Percentage of sexually active eighteen-year-olds in 1988: **74**
Percentage of sexually active eighteen-year-olds in 1999: **80**
[Sources: The Alan Guttmacher Institute/Rollin, L., 1999]

Percentage of nonvirgin American 12- to 14-year-olds: **20**
Percentage of 14-year-olds who have been to a party with alcohol: **50**
[Source: *The New York Times,* May 20, 2003]

Percentage of teenagers who have had sex without a condom while intoxicated: **20**
Percentage of teenagers who believe unprotected sex is not a "big deal": **17**
Percentage of teenagers who say alcohol has influenced their decision to do something sexual at least once: **25**
Percentage of 15- to 17-year-olds who believe "waiting to have sex is a nice idea but nobody really does it": **63**
[Source: The Kaiser Family Foundation, May 2003]

Percentage of high school seniors who have had four or more sexual partners: **21**
[Source: The American Academy of Pediatrics]

"After a half-century during which generations of young women were advised to never call a boy on the telephone, it is now teenage girls who not only do the calling, but who often initiate romantic and even sexual activity. Whether they are influenced by the trickle-down effects of feminism, which has taught girls to be assertive in all areas of life, or have internalized the images of sexually powerful women in popular culture, American girls are more daring than ever. . . . The teenage girl as sexual aggressor is a recurring character in music videos, almost macho in her pursuit of sex and advertising her pleasure in it."
—THE NEW YORK TIMES, NOVEMBER 3, 2002

JESSICA JONES, 13

RESTON, VIRGINIA

[Quoted from *A Tribe Apart:*
A Journey Into the Heart of American
Adolescence, Random House, 1999]

"It is like, when you go to a party and get drunk, you get horny. That is just what happens, and you hook up with people. Most people have sex . . ."

KAYLA B., 18

ST. PAUL, MINNESOTA

"I'm pretty sure his name started with 'L,' like Larry or Loren or something. Anyway, we had fun."

"Researchers in Washington, D.C. recently started a program to prevent early sexual activity. They planned to offer it to seventh-graders, but after a pilot study decided to target fifth-graders—too many seventh-graders were having sex.... 'The other day at school a girl got caught in the bathroom with a boy performing oral sex on him,' says Maurisha Stenson, a 14-year-old eighth-grader at a Syracuse, N.Y., middle school."

—USA TODAY, MARCH 14, 2002

ASHLEY O., 19

WASHINGTON, D.C.

"It's kind of annoying when you get too drunk to remember the guy's name the morning after you hook up or whatever. I mean, like, I guess it's not the worst thing in the world to forget, but it's still kind of annoying."

JULIAN H., 18

NEW YORK CITY

"I just turned 18 and I'm in college. I've hooked up with many girls at my school and more than once I didn't know their names. The funny thing is that there's always that conflict between my penis and my brain, but unfortunately my penis always wins. I never got to have sex so I'm in that weird group of eighteen-year-olds who are virgins, but I've also done everything else, with my longest relationship being two weeks."

"By the age of 14, more than half of all boys have touched a girl's breasts, and a quarter have touched a girl's vulva. One half of young people report experience with fellatio and cunnilingus."
—SEXUAL TEENS, SEXUAL MEDIA: INVESTIGATING MEDIA'S INFLUENCE ON ADOLESCENT SEXUALITY, EDITED BY JANE D. BROWN, JEANNE R. STEELE AND KIM WALSH-CHILDERS, LAWRENCE ERLBAUM ASSOCIATES, 2002

"cunnilingus \ n : oral stimulation of the vulva or clitoris."
—THE NEW MERRIAM-WEBSTER DICTIONARY

JENNIFER C., 18

PHILADELPHIA,
PENNSYLVANIA

"I've been hooking up with this guy for the last few weeks, and I really, really like him, but I know he's been having sex with this other girl. And I'm not conservative at all, but I told him it bothers me that he's hooking up with someone else. He just said that if I want anything from him at all, I shouldn't make demands."

MY MAKE-OUT SESSION WITH WATERMELON TITS

A Pathetic Memoir

"Girls worried [in the 1950s] about how to keep a boy's respect and still let him 'do what he wants to do.' ... Boys were expected to pressure girls gradually for more and more favors, while girls— at least, those who wanted to appear 'nice' and continue to get dates and steadies—allowed only so much and no more.... Such a system inevitably led to bewilderment and frustration for both."

—TWENTIETH-CENTURY TEEN CULTURE BY THE DECADES: A REFERENCE GUIDE BY LUCY ROLLIN, GREENWOOD PRESS, 1999

"Although this book is intended for the enjoyment of boys and girls ...part of my plan has been to pleasantly remind adults of what they once were themselves, and of how they felt and thought and talked, and what queer enterprises they sometimes engaged in."

—THE ADVENTURES OF TOM SAWYER BY MARK TWAIN, 1876

January 18, 2000

"Is this the right house?" I ponder aloud, nervously steering the 1984 Dodge MiniVan into the Girl's driveway. I've never actually been on a blind date in all my sixteen years on Planet Earth, and the anxiety brought on by this grim reality is crippling to say the least. After all, tonight will be nothing less than a veritable test of my *entire personality*. Good Lord, how could I *not* be terrified? Questions and Doubts, Questions and Doubts:

Am I her type of guy?

Is she my type of girl?

What if I *am* her type of guy?

And what if she's *my* type of girl? What then?

Or what if I'm *not* her type of guy and she's not my type of girl and tonight just turns out to be an incredibly awkward Torture Session for the both of us?

Does she bite while giving head?

The front door of the house suddenly opens and out walks the Girl: Brunette, five-foot-five (my height exactly), skintight blue T-shirt and Jesus of Nazareth, are those Gazongas ever *plump*. Christ, how can she even *walk* with those things? *Wow!* I mean, Good Fucking *God!* You'll be mine soon enough, Little Pretties. Just you fucking wait.

"Hi," Watermelon Tits says, opening the maroon door and entering the Love Mobile.[1] "I'm [Ms. Tits]."

"What's up?" I ask, trying and failing to sound the least bit cool. "I'm Marty. Hey, you look great."

Those Rotund Fucking Orbs of yours, that is. *Fuck!*

"Oh . . ." She closes the door and buckles her maroon seatbelt. "Thanks."

"So," I say, backing the MiniVan out of the driveway, "have you heard much about this movie we're seeing?"

"Not really . . ."

She sounds nervous as well. Perfectly understandable, of course: Why, she's probably having the exact same doubts *I* am! Ha! Who would've thought? (Well, bitch best put out if bitch knows what's best for bitch.)

"This is a pretty cool ride you've got here," the Girl heartlessly and needlessly insults the Love Mobile.

"This van is so lame," I confess. "I mean, my parents gave it to me for free—so it's not like I'm complaining or anything—but girls think it's creepy and guys think it's pathetic, and I'm not exactly arguing."

"Why don't you buy your own car?" she asks.

"Why don't you suck my own cock?" I mutter.

"What?" she barks. *"What did you just say?"*

"I said it's six o'clock. We're going to miss the movie previews."

"Oh . . ." she says. "Well, hurry up."

Obedient as always, I accelerate the MiniVan from twenty miles per hour to sixty-five: The perfect speed for any child-ridden residential neighborhood. We soon arrive at the crowded theater and—after finding a parking space conveniently located eighty-five million miles from the actual theater entrance—buy tickets and find seats that, judging from the general lukewarm stickiness, have been freshly ejaculated upon. The movie, your standard romantic comedy, has already started.

---

1 / In the interest of literary timelessness, it should be noted that the 1984 Dodge MiniVan is quite possibly the single most pathetic, effeminate and hideous automobile ever crafted by Man. In this nation (America), where the average teenage boy can easily coax sex from the average teenage girl assuming he owns even a mildly impressive automobile, driving a 1984 Dodge MiniVan is akin to severing one's own Teenage Penis with an Axe.

"Um, [Ms. Tits]?" I whisper after a few moments, my voice inevitably cracking like it hasn't since I first entered puberty. "Can I put my arm around you?"

Please, Lord Jesus? Please, please, please?

"You're not supposed to *ask*." She blushes.

Praise Heaven! Praise Allah! Praise the LORD!

The next ninety minutes pass all too quickly, Watermelon Tits' warm, voluptuous body pressed so close to mine that I'm unable to focus on anything but keeping my Hungry Hard-On at bay. Goodness Gracious, I'm going to enjoy licking those Fatty Fun Bags till they fucking *erode.*

"So how did you like the movie?" I ask on our trek back to the Love Mobile.

"It was okay," Watermelon Tits says, putting her hand in mine. "I liked when [blah, blah, blah, blah, blah, blah, blah]."

"Cool . . . So, um . . . Do you want to go anywhere else now?"

"Actually my parents kind of want me home before curfew."

"Well, I'm sure they'll already be asleep by then."

"I know, I know. I'm sorry. I just have to get home."

"Okay, okay, sure, fine, whatever." I fight back an ocean of tears.

We take our respective seats in the MiniVan and drive in silence back to her affluent Anchorage neighborhood.

"Which street do I turn on?" I ask, approaching a four-way intersection.

"Right there." She points toward a narrow dirt road past the crossing.

"Hey, what would you say if I asked whether or not you'd want me to pull into that dark spot on the side of the road there so we could make out or whatever?"

Okay, what in the fucking Hell did you just say, Beckerman? I ask myself. You're an idiot. Do you know that? Not to mention fucking hopeless. Those Meaty Jugamajiggies will never be yours now, fool! Never! Never! Never!

"You're not supposed to *ask*." She blushes again.

"Really?" I grin with succulent expectation and park the MiniVan. "I mean . . . like . . . *really?"*

"Really." She smiles the most precious giant breasts. I mean "smile." Ha! Ha!

"You're going to love this." I unbuckle my maroon seat belt and lean over to kiss her pleading teenage lips.

"Wait . . ." She places her hands on my shoulders and ruins the moment.

"Wait?" I scream. *"We don't have time to fucking wait! My scrotum is about to burst!"*

"This is my first kiss."

Oh, no . . . No, no, no, no. *No.* Not now. Not when I'm so, so *close.*

"Maybe we shouldn't then," I sigh.

"I *want* to," she says. "It's just—"

"It's your *first kiss.* You deserve better. Seriously, it's supposed to be special."

"Ohhhhh, you're sweet." She inches closer and closer. (Yeah, Motherfucker: Those Mondo Milk Producers are *Mine! Mine!* All Fucking *Mine!*) "That was different than I thought it would be," she says after the kiss has come to its natural conclusion.

"You didn't like it?" I question both her and my masculinity.

"I *did* like it," she confesses. "I just always thought it would feel . . . I don't know . . . different."

"Don't worry about it."

I lean in again and—like any real man—waste no time in slipping her the Tongue. She seems a bit taken aback by this turn of events, and unfortunately for my digestive system doesn't understand her end of the bargain.

"You're supposed to move it around," I explain.

"I'm supposed to move what around?"

"Your tongue," I elucidate. "You're supposed to move your tongue around. In circles."

"Um . . . Sorry?"

"You weren't moving it around. That was disgusting."

"I . . . I'm sorry . . . I didn't *know.*"

"That's right. You didn't know. And maybe that's why you just let your tongue hang in my mouth like a wet shrimp or an octopus tentacle or . . . or *something*. Christ."

"I didn't *know*," she whimpers. "I didn't—"

"It's okay," I console, leaning in once again.

Yes, the Meaty Jugamajiggies are right there in front of me—so firm and yet so *soft*—all but awaiting the Gratifying Grope of my sweaty Jewish palms.

Now, how do I go about making the move? I ponder while swirling my tongue within her sweet mouth. *Perhaps I should say something romantic! Ah, that's it! I'm a genius!*

"So can I touch your boobies now?" I woo.

"Home," Watermelon Tits says.

"What?" I ask.

"Home. Take me home."

"I was just joking," I lie. "Ha! Ha!"

"Home," she says. "Now."

"You know you don't mean that."

"Didn't you *hear* me? Home."

"Okay, okay, sure, fine, whatever."

And thus tonight's whorish exploit ends. The Meaty Jugamajiggies may as well have been in the farthest regions of Deep Space all along, for neither shall ever know the Agonizing Pleasure of Marty Beckerman's Lecherous Squeeze. Oh well, her loss.

"Please?" I ask.

"No," she says.

"You shouldn't play with people's fucking *emotions* like that," I weep. "Shit, I cared about you and all you did was *use* me. I have feelings *too*, you know. It's not like I'm a piece of fucking *meat*."

"Home," she says. "Now."

↗ S.L.U.T. STATS

14,000:

Sexual references the average teenager views on television per year.
[Source: The American Academy of Pediatrics]

28:

Hours the average child spends watching television per week.
[Source: The American Academy of Pediatrics]

64%:

Percentage of American teenagers who have a television set in their bedrooms.
[Source: *Up from Invisibility* by Larry Gross, Columbia University Press, 2001]

72%:

Percentage of American teenagers that believe sexual behaviors on television influence the sexual behaviors of other teenagers 'somewhat' or 'a lot.'
[Source: The Kaiser Family Foundation, July 2002]

223,673:

Number of American teenagers who received cosmetic plastic surgery in 2002.
[Source: The American Society of Plastic Surgeons, April 2003]

"Parents wondering if their teenagers are having sex might look upstairs or down the hall. New research finds most sexually active teens first had sex in their parents' homes, typically late at night.... 'Kids no longer need to drive to [the] lookout point to have sex,' said Sarah Brown, director of the National Campaign to Prevent Teen Pregnancy. The data suggest the adults may be in the house."
—THE ASSOCIATED PRESS, SEPTEMBER 26, 2002

"COLDWATER, Mich.—A 17-year-old is charged with a felony for allegedly having unprotected sex with a local man without telling him she has AIDS. Prosecutors charged Amber Jo Sours with the four-year felony after police identified four men who claimed they had sex with her and didn't know she carries the disease.... The 17-year-old smiled and laughed when informed of the charge in court Monday.... Sours has been in the juvenile court system since she gave birth to a child at the age of 12."
—THE ASSOCIATED PRESS, MARCH 6, 2003

"Last month, the Alan Guttmacher Institute published the first national study to look at the sexual practices of adolescent boys, ages 15 to 19. Researchers found that while 55 percent of boys in this age group claimed to have had vaginal intercourse, two-thirds of the boys surveyed said they had engaged in oral sex, anal sex or 'masturbation by a female.' More than one in 10 boys had engaged in anal sex, half had received oral sex from a girl and slightly more than a third had performed oral sex on a girl. What's more, many of these teens said they do not consider oral or even anal sex to be sex—some even called it 'abstinence.'"
—SALON.COM, JANUARY 10, 2001

"Students at Palo Alto High are about to learn that 'freaking'—a popular way of dancing that simulates sex-will get them kicked out of school dances.... Principal Sandra Pearson plans to tell the school's 1,650 students today that she is banning sexually provocative dance moves in response to suggestions from some parents and students. Freaking, however, isn't like the Twist. 'It's different because there are instances when a girl will be on the floor and there will be guys on top of her,' rising and falling in sync with the song, Pearson explained. And there are times when a student's head is nuzzled in another's crotch. Or legs are hung around hips as pelvises thrust against each other. 'I don't understand why it's an issue,' said Blake, 16. 'You have four layers of clothing between you.'"
—THE MERCURY NEWS, FEBRUARY 20, 2003

"For high school teens (in the 1920s), dating behavior was somewhat constrained by the proximity to home.... The 'petting party'
was the most notorious arena for testing sexual feelings and
responses. During the decade, 'necking' came to refer to ardent
and prolonged kissing, while 'petting' described many kinds of
erotic activity, but usually referred to caresses and fondling
below the neck. At petting parties, where couples engaged in these
activities with other couples nearby, the group nature of the
event provided automatic limits on how far to go."
—TWENTIETH-CENTURY TEEN CULTURE BY THE DECADES: A REFERENCE GUIDE BY LUCY
ROLLIN, GREENWOOD PRESS, 1999

"KINGSTON, Mass.—A Silver Lake Regional High School teacher says
that, contrary to police reports, the two teenagers who allegedly
engaged in a sex act on a school bus last month were not cheered
on by other riders. 'From the briefing, it was my understanding
the kids were just watching and didn't know what else to do,'
said Craig Brown, a high school math teacher."
—THE BOSTON GLOBE, JANUARY 11, 2003

SATURDAY

"Oh... sorry. But it's Max. Not Mike or Rex or . . . Hello? Ashley? Hello?"

"For the love of God, Brett, it's two-thirty in the afternoon." Mr. Hunter opened the bedroom door and shook his son awake. "I want to know how late you were up last night."

"Oh Christ, Dad." Brett groaned. "Let me sleep."

"You're sixteen years old, Brett. Do you think Trevor Thompson became the pride and joy of this town by *sleeping* until three in the afternoon? What about your brother? Do you think he would've gotten that scholarship to Oregon if he'd stayed in bed all day?"

"I don't know. . . . He's in bed all day now, isn't he?"

"Shut up, now. You've got thirty minutes to get the driveway shoveled, and I suggest you get straight to work if you feel like going to your prom tonight."

"What if I *don't* want to go to the stupid prom? Then I don't have to shovel the stupid driveway?"

"Let me rephrase that. If you fail to clear the driveway in the next half hour, I'll fail to provide you with dinner and a bed tonight."

"Like Mom would ever let you kick me out of the house." Brett rolled over on the mattress. "Where's Max?"

"I drove him to his parents' apartment three hours ago. He threw up in the backseat."

"Oh, really? He must've caught that flu going around school. He felt pretty sick last night."

"Don't give me that bullshit when you've got four empty beer bottles lying on your floor." Mr. Hunter closed the bedroom door. "Twenty-eight minutes on the driveway."

"She doesn't . . . doesn't . . ." Max stood on the rooftop of the thirteen-story apartment complex, looking down at the busy street below. "She doesn't even remember my *name.*"

The stairwell door opened. A crimson-haired girl walked onto the roof.

"Wow," she said. "Nice view."

"Yeah." Max wiped the tears off his cheeks. "Actually if you spit off the edge there and it lands on someone's head, they'll be killed instantly."

"Okay . . . Why would you want to do *that?*"

"Well, God, I've never actually *tried* it."

"That's probably a good thing." She smiled. "Hi, I'm Julia. I just moved in today from Anchorage . . . Apartment ten-thirteen?"

"Really? *Alaska?* Wow. You're right across the hall from me. I'm Max, by the way."

"Nice to meet you. So do you go to Kapkovian Pacific?"

"Oh, yeah. It's okay for a school, I guess. You're going there?"

"Starting Monday. I'm kind of nervous about it, to be honest."

"Don't worry. You're like a sophomore or junior or—"

"Freshman. Well, I mean, I'm not a *man,* but—"

"Damnit." Max clenched his fists. "I had you *pegged* for a man."

"Sorry." She laughed. "So do you come up here to the roof a lot?"

"Sometimes. It's a pretty good place to think about stuff."

"Really? What do you usually think about?"

"How much being short sucks. . . . What happened to *X-Files* the last couple seasons . . . Stuff like that, I guess."

"Why don't you like being short?"

"It's an evolutionary thing. Like, you're less of a man because there's less of you, so you're the weaker animal in the food chain or something, not to mention less desirable for mating. Girls always dream about Mr. *Tall* and Handsome, right?"

"I don't know. Usually I dream about running away from aliens."

"Never mind, I guess. So what kind of music do you listen to?"

"Oh, I don't know. I like everything."

"Come on. Nobody likes *everything.*"

"Well . . . it's kind of embarrassing."

"What? Gospel? Country?"

"Promise you won't laugh?"

"I promise I won't laugh."

"Okay . . . Oldies. Don't *laugh*."

"I'm not." Max laughed. "So do you like the Beatles?"

"I *love* the Beatles. All my friends tease me for it though."

"Really? My friend Brett calls them 'the Faggles' actually . . . So what's your favorite song?"

"Well, it was 'Hey Jude' for the longest time, but then George died from cancer and I put on *Abbey Road* and listened to 'Something'—I mean the song, 'Something,' not just *something*—and I just started crying because nothing had ever made me feel that happy and that sad at the same time, and I couldn't stop thinking about how he must've had so much love in him to write something that beautiful. And I thought about how I hope I can have that much love in me too someday and how I want to write something that beautiful, but I don't know if I can because I don't really know anything about how to write lyrics or music or anything like that. . . . Sorry, what's your favorite song, Max?"

"That's easy." He smiled. " 'Julia.'"

"Oh . . ." She blushed. "Good choice."

"Do you ever think about how the Beatles could just be forgotten someday? I mean, millions of people know their songs by heart and everything, but in the cosmic scheme of things, do you think that thirty or forty or a thousand years from now people might not even know who the Beatles *were* because their songs just won't *relate* to anyone anymore?"

"I don't know . . . *We* weren't alive when they recorded all their music, but we still listen to them, right? Why shouldn't people a thousand years from now?"

"I guess that makes sense. I don't know, sometimes I just think about how if the human race died out then all our books and music would just be forgotten like they never existed in the first place. And if they never existed, they never even made a difference."

"So do you think about the end of the world a lot?"

"Only when I don't want to do my homework, I guess."

"That's probably healthier than thinking about it all the time." She laughed. "Besides, all that stuff obviously *does* exist in the first place since we're talking about it right now. And if it makes a difference in people's lives now, then it has all the meaning in the world, don't you think?"

"Wow, Julia, you're like the deepest person in the world. . . . So have you ever been to another country or anything?"

"Well, I . . . I don't want to sound like I'm bragging."

"Okay . . . but—?"

"Well, Italy, Spain, France, um, England . . ."

"Oh my God, that's actually really impress—"

"Mexico, Iceland, Brazil, China, Japan, Hong Kong, Australia and New Zealand. Oh, Antarctica too, but I'm not sure whether or not that counts as a country."

"Whoa." Max laughed. "I've got Canada on my list and that's about it. So are your parents flight attendants or something?"

"No . . . they used to be in business."

"So they're moving in too, right?"

"Oh . . . um . . . no. I mean, not . . . no."

"Okay . . . so you're here all by *yourself?*"

"Please let's not talk about my parents, Max."

"Um . . . okay . . ." He bit his lower lip. "So you're not busy tonight, are you? Because I was just wondering if . . . I mean, I know you wouldn't really know too many people there or anything, but Kapkovian's winter prom is tonight and I won a couple tickets and I don't know if you'd want to go or anything but I *do* have those tickets and was just kind of wondering if maybe you'd like to—"

"Sure, Max." Julia smiled. "I'd love to."

"Come on, come on, come *on,*" Brett said into the telephone, lying on his bed and banging on the nightstand. "Pick up, pick up, pick—"

Hey, this is Quinn. Leave me a message after the beep and I'll get back to you as soon as I can. Beeeeeeeeeeep.

"Hey, it's Brett. You there? Quinn? Give me a call sometime, all right? I'm sorry about last night, it's just that I *know* something about Trevor and I don't want to see you get—" *Beeeeeeeeeeep.* "Fucked." He sighed and set the telephone down.

"Hey, Brett!" Max knocked on the windowsill. "Do you have an extra suit I could borrow?"

"What? You're going to *prom?*" Brett snickered. "That's a laugh."

"Well, I won those tickets and I wasn't planning on going except I just met this girl on my roof who moved into the apartment across from mine but I don't have any dress clothes and it's too late to rent a tux and I don't even have *money* to rent a tux and I'm getting kind of desperate so if you have an extra suit or anything like that I'd—"

"All right, all right. Settle down, fucker." Brett opened his clothes closet. "So this girl, she's cute or what?"

"She's *awesome.* She's from *Alaska* and she's traveled all over the *world* and she likes the *Beatles.*"

"She listens to the Faggles too?" Brett handed Max a dark gray suit through the window. "Shit. You're perfect for each other."

"Thanks a lot, Brett. Hey, did you ever ask Quinn to prom?"

"No . . . She's going with that fag writer Trevor Thompson."

"Holy crap. Isn't he on the cover of *Time* this week?"

"Fuck, man, I don't know." Brett sighed. "Probably."

"Wow, I'm sorry. That really sucks. You'll find another girl though, right? I mean, you're *you.*"

"Whatever . . . Prom's stupid anyway. Just one more bullshit excuse to get wasted and fuck some drunk slut, you know?"

"Oh . . . Well, I should probably go buy flowers for Julia." Max tucked the suit under his arm. "Thanks again, Brett. You're the best friend in the world."

"All right, fucker. Need a condom?"

"God, Brett. I just met this girl *today.*"

"Sure, sure." Brett smirked. "Whatever you say, tiger."

Beeeeeeep!

"Hello?" Brett picked up the telephone.

"Hey, Brett? It's Quinn. What's your fucking problem with Trevor? Would you stop being jealous of every other boy I date now that I broke up with you?"

"Listen to me, Quinn. Don't go out with that psychotic fuck-up, all right?"

"Brett, I really need to get back to putting on makeup for tonight. God, I haven't even *started* on my hair."

"I'm *serious,* Quinn. You're going to get seriously hurt. You have *no idea* what you're getting yourself into."

"Stop, Brett. I thought we decided we're better off as *friends with benefits,* remember? And obviously I like Trevor now, so would you please just get *over* me? I'll give you a call tomorrow."

"*Whatever.*" Brett hurled the telephone against the wall. "*Cunt.*"

Trevor took Quinn's hand and walked her to the driveway, then unlocked the passenger side door of his $137,000 silver 2003 BMW Z8 Roadster. "You really do look great tonight, Quinn. I can't tell you how happy I am that you see me in the same light that I do."

"Thanks for inviting me, Trevor." She stepped into the car. "You look great too."

"Oh, I know." He turned the key in the ignition.

"Oh my *God*. How much did this car *cost?*"

"Would you believe a half-million dollars?" He took the BMW from zero to seventy miles per hour in four seconds. "Hey Quinn, you don't think anyone would mind if we go fifty over the speed limit through your sweet little neighborhood, do you?"

"*Oh my God!*" she screamed. "*Wooooooo-hooooooooo!*"

"Zero to one hundred in less than six seconds." Trevor grinned. "You want to go to the Point before dinner?"

"*Forget it, Trevor. I'll suck your dick right here.*"

"Huh." He unzipped his fly midturn. "Good call."

"Hey, Julia?" Max stood in the hallway between his and her apartments, knocking on her front door. "Are you ready?"

"One second, Max." She frantically looked herself over in the bedroom mirror. "I'll be right out."

"Okay . . . I've got your cleavage right here whenever you're ready."

"*What?*" She darted into the hallway wearing a scarlet dress with silver evening sandals. "You have my *what?*"

"Well, I didn't know how big you wanted it or if it's supposed to be white or pink or whatever, but it's not like I buy cleavages every day so you'll have to forgive me."

"That's a *corsage,* Max." She rolled her eyes and took the flower wristband. "A cleavage is the depression between a girl's breasts when they're pressed together."

"Oh . . ." Max gulped. "Wow . . . that's, that's just . . . yeah, I'm a real idiot."

"No, you're not." She slipped the corsage over her wrist. "So where should we go for dinner?"

"There's this pretty good Mexican place a few blocks away, if you're into Mexican people at all."

"Do they have anything without meat?"

"Without *meat?* You're a *vegetarian?*"

"Of course." She smiled. "Aren't you?"

"Oh, right. . . . Let's go eat some *lettuce.*"

They took the elevator down to the main lobby and soon arrived at El Hombre del Mar Authentic Mexican Cuisine. The restaurant smelled of ground beef and piquant salsa; nearly every table was occupied. Max opened the door and followed Julia inside, then approached the Hispanic waitress behind the reservations podium.

"*Hola,*" the waitress said. "Party of two?"

"Right," Max said. "We're vegetarians."

"Right this way." She led Max and Julia to a small table near the back of the restaurant. "Would you like anything to drink before ordering?"

"I'll just have a glass of water, please," Julia said.

"Yes." Max opened the leatherette menu. "I'll have your nation of origin's pathetic little Third World economy, with a shot of famine and two twists of inexpensive child labor. *En un cubilete frío, tu perra gorda.*" [1]

"*What?*" the waitress shrieked. "*What did you just say?*"

"I'll have a Sprite, please," Max clarified. "*Gracias.*"

"Oh . . ." She penned the order in her notepad. "Okay."

"What was *that* all about, Max?" Julia asked. "You're not a *racist,* are you?"

"No, no, no. I—I was just trying to be funny like my friend Brett, but I don't think it worked very well and I'm sorry and I'll just be myself now."

"*Oh fuck, oh God, oh God, Quinn,*" Trevor squealed, muscles tensed and eyes closed, taking the BMW to its maximum velocity on the open expressway. "Let's not even *go* to the fucking prom."

---

1 / "In a frosty mug, you fatty bitch."

"So why aren't you going to the prom tonight, honey?" Mrs. Hunter asked, placing the serving dish of asparagus and chicken Parmesan onto the glass dinner table. "You were so excited for winter prom last year, don't you remember?"

"No." Brett folded a napkin over his lap.

"You could've gone with Quinn Kaysen again, couldn't you? You two were so cute together last year. Weren't they cute together, dear?"

"Good looking couple, you two." Mr. Hunter took a bite of the chicken Parmesan. "Gorgeous young lady, that Kaysen girl."

"She's going with Trevor Thompson tonight." Brett speared the asparagus with his fork. "Apparently they're exclusive now or something."

"Well, good for her." Mr. Hunter took another bite. "I keep telling you, Brett, that Thompson boy is *going* somewhere. He's a kid this whole *community* can be proud of—just like your brother. You should try being more like him."

"Do you remember when you chased Quinn around the playground in kindergarten?" Mrs. Hunter smiled. "Her parents would call us every night complaining about how you'd tried to kiss her. And then one horrible day she kicked you right between the—"

"Oh God, Mom," Brett groaned. "Could you possibly *be* any more embarrassing?"

Silence.

"Listen, I'm sorry . . . Mom, please, I'm . . . Mom, Mom please . . ."

"You never speak to your mother like that again, goddamnit." Mr. Hunter banged the glass table with his fists. *"Do you hear me, Brett? Do you fucking hear me? Goddamnit, you better fucking hear me this time."*

"Okay, I've got another question." Julia dipped a tortilla chip into the complimentary mild salsa. "Do you believe in unconditional love?"

"I don't know," Max said. "What's unconditional love?"

"Well, I'm not sure if it would be like soulmates or anything because I'm not even sure if I believe in souls, but maybe something more like *synchronicity,* you know? Like how certain people are just supposed to be together, so they'll find each other no matter what?"

"Maybe, I guess . . . I mean, sometimes I think that everyone's personality is kind of like a pyramid or something, you know? All the older experiences are at the base and the newer experiences are at the top, so even though you add new experiences all the time, you'll always be the same person deep down. And I think if you fall in love with someone and they fall in love with you, then a part of you will always care about them because no matter what happens those parts will always be there, even though things might change on the surface."

"That's really deep, Max. I'm so happy you're able to think like that."

The waitress placed a glass of ice water in front of Julia and a glass of Sprite in front of Max. He withdrew the plastic straw and laid it on the ceramic plate.

"Not a straw person?" Julia asked. "That's weird."

"Brett says that straight guys can't drink out of straws."

"And why exactly *can't* straight guys drink from straws?"

"Ready to order?" the waitress asked, uncapping her pen.

"Could I have the veggie taco salad?" Julia asked. "No cheese, please."

"Muy bien." The waitress wrote the order down. "And for you, sir?"

"I'll have the chicken enchilada combo." Max handed the leatherette menus back to the waitress. "Thanks a lot."

"Some vegetarian." Julia rolled her eyes.

"Oh, did I say I was a *vegetarian?* Well, see, what I *meant* was I'd *be* a vegetarian if I actually had any *willpower.* Um . . . Sorry for the confusion and everything."

"It's not about *willpower,* Max. It's about being *disgusted* by the idea of eating *animals.*"

"God, Julia, it's not *my* fault those innocent little critters taste so good."

"So would you eat a *dog* if it tasted good?"

"No!" Max shrieked. "I *love* my dog."

"Then why would you eat a chicken?"

"I don't know. Chickens are stupid and dogs are cool."

"So you base what you will and won't eat on how *cool* it is before it's *dead?*"

"Okay, okay, sure, fine, whatever." Max hailed the waitress back to the table. "Ma'am, could I actually change my order to the veggie taco salad? Without cheese? And don't forget the lettuce."

"So who do we have on the menu tonight?" Brett stood over his Sony Vaio laptop, logging onto Yahoo! Personals and filling out the multichoice form boxes:

I'M A: MAN SEEKING A: WOMAN
Age: 14 to 18
Within: 20 MILES

He clicked on "Find My Match" and waited for the search engine to process the query. A list of fifty girls soon appeared, a description and photograph beside each.

"So many vaginas, so little time." He scanned over the listings and clicked on the fifteenth down:

```
"Sexy beast looking for a fun guy!"
Age: 16
Looking for: Friends * Just Dating * Intimate/Physical
Ethnicity: Caucasian (White)
Hair: Light brown
Education: High school
Religion: Catholic
Interests: Dancing * Movies * Music * Outdoor Activities * Sports
```

"Good enough." Brett copied down the girl's AOL Instant Messenger screen name and opened that application:

```
KAPKOV_TRACK_CHAMP69: 'Sup?
SUNNYHOURZGIRL1987: Who r u?
KAPKOV_TRACK_CHAMP69: 16/m, saw your pic on yahoo, you're super-cute!
SUNNYHOURZGIRL1987: thanx . . .
KAPKOV_TRACK_CHAMP69: so why are you @ home sat. night?
SUNNYHOURZGIRL1987: parents took the car to some movie, zzzzzzzzz.
KAPKOV_TRACK_CHAMP69: all alone?
SUNNYHOURZGIRL1987: Just doing homework . . . You have a pic?
KAPKOV_TRACK_CHAMP69: One sec.
```

Brett opened the digital folder "My Pictures" and attached a scanned photograph into his next message.

```
KAPKOV_TRACK_CHAMP69: Look familiar?
SUNNYHOURZGIRL1987: didn't the sports page have a big thing on u last week?
KAPKOV_TRACK_CHAMP69: Bingo.
SUNNYHOURZGIRL1987: coooool . . . so why are u @ home?
KAPKOV_TRACK_CHAMP69: Asshole took my girlfriend to prom.
```

```
SUNNYHOURZGIRL1987: wow . . . some girlfriend.
KAPKOV_TRACK_CHAMP69: well . . . ex-girlfriend I guess.
SUNNYHOURZGIRL1987: that sux!! so ur on the rebound?
KAPKOV_TRACK_CHAMP69: What can I say? your pic is CUTE!!!!
SUNNYHOURZGIRL1987: k . . . meet outside spring grove mall in 15 min.?
KAPKOV_TRACK_CHAMP69: cool . . . cya soon . . . I'll b the guy w/ no
shirt.
SUNNYHOURZGIRL1987: all right . . . lol!
```

"Mom, I'm heading out!" Brett turned off the computer and sprinted outside to his Camry. He sped to the shopping center, removing his T-shirt once in the parking lot. A sandy-haired girl stood alone by the front entrance. He rolled down the passenger side window. "So your parents never warned you about all the fucking perverts on the Internet?"

"Oh my God." The girl laughed. "I can't *believe* you actually came without your *shirt.*"

"You must be freezing. Come on in, I don't bite."

She opened the car door and took a seat inside.

"So you're a freshman or sophomore?" Brett asked.

"Sophomore." She rolled up the window. "You?"

"Sophomore." He steered the Camry behind the mall. "And you like oral sex?"

"Wow. *You're* up-front." She blushed. "Well, it depends. Am I giving or getting?"

"Getting. No girls anywhere *like* giving. Or swallowing."

"God, are we *supposed* to? I mean, *guys* don't need to swallow anything when you go down on *us.*"

"Well, it's not exactly paradise down there either. I still fucking love it though. I mean, girls really like getting it, and I think the female orgasm should always come first."

"Really? That's so sweet. God, I just don't understand why all guys *insist* we have to swallow."

"It's a psychological thing, you know? You can always just come in her mouth without telling her it's going to happen, but then you feel kind of guilty inside. And who needs *that* right after an orgasm?"

"Up-front *and* honest." She laughed. "So why are we talking about this again?"

"I don't know." Brett leaned in and kissed her. "Maybe we shouldn't talk anymore?"

They fondled their way to the backseat, removing all significant articles of clothing in the process.

"You have *such* a nice body." She slipped her hand inside Brett's boxers. "When you pulled up without your shirt, I swear to God I got wet just like *that.*"

"Yeah?" He smirked and closed his eyes. "Christ, I need this so bad. You wouldn't *believe* the shit my ex is putting me through."

She unzipped his fly and pulled his penis out of his plaid boxers.

"So if I promise to swallow, will you spank me for a little while?"

"You're *kidding,* right?" He laughed. "You want to be *spanked?*"

"Um-hmm." She slid her body over Brett's lap. "It's my favorite thing to do."

"Ooookay . . . So am I supposed to pull your panties down first or—?"

Beeeeeeep!

"One second." Brett reached for his cell phone on the dashboard. *"Yeah?"*

"I'm going fucking insane, Brett. Oh God, I think I'm going fucking *crazy.*"

"Ash? Is that you? Listen, I'm kind of in the middle of something. I'll give you a call back as soon as I get home, all right?"

"No, Brett. Tell me not to do it. Tell me I'm not crazy. Tell me not to kill my—"

Brett turned off the phone and pulled the girl's pink panties down to her knees. "Now where were we again?"

"So here we are, I guess." Max opened the gymnasium door and marveled at the hundreds of students inside, all wearing tuxedos and three-hundred-dollar dresses.

"Wow . . ." Julia said. "So many *people.*"

Balloons and ribbons dangled from the basketball hoops on each side of the gymnasium; hundreds of candles glowed on round tables encircling the makeshift dance floor; teachers and parents stood at all the exits, ensuring that no students sneaked out to procure drugs or alcohol; under the steel bleachers, myriad circles of students briskly chugged from small flasks and inhaled from packed rolling papers.

"So do you want to go dance now?" Julia asked.

"Maybe we could get something to drink first?"

"Okay. Sure." She followed Max to the concession table, gazing at the countless couples freak-dancing in the strobe lights. "Do you ever feel like they're all just a different species?"

"Brett says they're all scared of each other for some reason." Max poured two glasses of fruit punch. "But I don't really understand, because I wouldn't be scared of too much if I were tall and played sports and people liked me."

"I don't think I'd be very scared either if I looked like those girls . . . Is Brett into sports or something?"

"He's a runner. He actually wins a lot of races for the school and I guess that's why so many people like him, but I think deep down he wishes they just liked him for who he really—"

The hired deejay suddenly played the Beatles'"Let It Be."[2] The freak dancing morphed into *slow* freak dancing.

"Please, Max?" Julia motioned toward the dance floor. "Pleeeeaase?"

"Yeah, um, here's the thing. And I know I'm a really bad prom date and I should've told you this before and I'm sorry I didn't, but I can't . . . Julia, I can't dance."

"You mean you get too self-conscious? I'm sure it's not *that* bad."

"No, I mean I physically *can't dance.* At least not without looking like a hippopotamus dying from some kind of severe leg wound or something."

"Okay . . . So why did you even ask me here tonight?"

"I . . . I don't know . . . It seemed like a good idea at the time."

"Come *on.*" She smiled and held out her hands. "I promise I won't laugh."

"Oh, fine." Max nervously led her onto the balloon-replete dance floor. She put her arms around his shoulders. He put his around her back. They rotated in no particular cadence for the next four minutes, bumping into other couples and stepping on each other's toes.

"How was that?" Max asked once the song had finished.

"It was great. You didn't look like a dying hippopotamus."

"Awesome. . . . You look really, really beautiful tonight, Julia."

"Oh . . ." She reddened. "Okay."

And Max knew one thing:

This had to be love.

"I'm a fucking whore." Ashley stood naked facing the bathroom mirror. "Just this little fucking slut." She opened the medicine cabinet and removed her mother's orange vials of prescription painkillers, sleeping pills and antidepressants. "And they fuck me and I let them fuck me and I don't even like it, but does anyone ask me to prom?" She twisted the plastic caps off the vials and filled her hands with seventy-seven white and yellow capsules. "Well, they'll be sorry." Tears streaked down her cheeks as she swallowed pill after pill after pill after pill. "They'll be so, so fucking sorry."

"Welcome home, Quinn." Trevor opened the front door of his penthouse apartment and waited for the infrared occupancy detector to illuminate the living room. "What do you think? Cozy little place? Shangri-La?"

2 / This would never actually happen, considering two of the most popular prom songs in recent history have been entitled "The Thong Song" and "Back That Ass Up."

"Oh my God." She tried to take it all in at once: The polished walnut floors; the tinted windows overlooking the downtown skyline; the $15,000 black leather couches; the imported surround-sound system; the wide-screen digital television; the various artwork procured from Tokyo and Cairo; the wall-mounted aquarium housing endangered specimens from across the globe. "This apartment is *amazing,* Trevor. Most *adults* couldn't afford a place like this."

"Modesty *is* for the weak, Quinn." He removed his tuxedo jacket and laid it on the leather sectional. "Most adults wouldn't have the taste anyway."

"How did you *do* this, Trevor? Last year you were just another *kid* and now you're so *confident* and *responsible.* It's like in that book we had to read for Ms. Lovelace, *The Great Gatsburg* or whatever it's called. Your parents aren't giving you your inheritance early or anything, are they?"

"My mother is already dead, Quinn." Trevor walked to the kitchen and opened a maple drawer. "The money came entirely from the late-nineties technology boom. Of course, the royalties from *Investing for Teenagers* don't hurt any. You'd assume the down market would actually *hurt* sales of an investment book, but people are looking for financial advice more than ever. They're *scared,* Quinn. Not just of economic downturn, but disease, terrorism, unending war, worldwide hatred against America. I've simply capitalized on this limitless fear. The rewards of ingenuity surround you."

"So what happened to your mom? I mean, if you're okay talking about it."

"Would you like anything to drink, Quinn?" Trevor placed his hand on the white bottle of Malibu coconut rum in the cedar drawer. "We've got cognac, scotch, bourbon, Malibu, peppermint schn—"

"Oh, I *love* Malibu," Quinn smiled, sitting down on the black leather couch. "Could you put any mixers in it?"

"Absolutely, Quinn." Trevor poured five shots of Malibu into a glass and mixed in lemon-lime soda from the refrigerator, then added twelve milligrams of gamma hydroxybutyrate from a vial hidden in his tuxedo pocket. He poured a separate glass of water from the kitchen sink and returned to the living room. "One Malibu with Sprite for the princess, and one glass of gin for the king."

"You're drinking straight *gin?*" Quinn laughed, sipping the Malibu. "Wow, Trevor, this is really great. You can't even *taste* the alcohol."

"I'm glad to hear that, Quinn." He sat on the black leather couch beside her. "I don't know about you, but I'm getting absolutely *smashed* tonight."

"Oh, don't worry about me." She gulped down the rum and soda. "Brett always calls me 'Two-Shot Quinn' for a reason."

"Christ, babe, why do you still spend *time* with that worthless jock playboy? You broke up with him so *we* could be together, remember?"

"We've been friends since *preschool,* Trevor. When we were little kids he actually tried to pin me down and kiss me all the time, but one day I kneed him right in the crotch and he never—"

"That would explain a lot." Trevor chugged the water, feigning revulsion at the taste. "Oh my *God,* Quinn, I'm getting so *buzzed.*"

"Oh God, me *too.*" She swallowed the last of the Malibu. "It tastes really good though."

"Have as much as you want, Quinn." Trevor walked to the kitchen and returned with the white bottle, then refilled her glass. "Don't be afraid to ask for more."

"You're such a sweetie, Trevor." She took a larger mouthful than she intended; the excess rum trickled down her chin and spilled onto her white prom dress. "Oh God, I . . . I think I'm starting to get really . . . realllllly . . ."

"You're doing fine, Quinn." Trevor refilled her glass again. "See?" He guzzled the tap water and then lifted Quinn's glass to her mouth. "*I'm* the one getting fucked-up here. You're holding yours fine."

"It's . . . it's all . . . sparkling?" She lost her balance and nearly fell off the black leather couch.

"Do you want to see the bedroom?" Trevor ran one finger up her white prom dress, lightly touching the edge of her Pike & Crew panties. He reached for the remote control on the glass coffee table and selected the Red Hot Chili Peppers' *Californication* from the five-hundred-disc changer.

"Oh, I *love* this . . . this *song,*" Quinn said, unable to open her eyes. "You . . . you like this . . . this sonnnnnnnnnnnnng?"

"Of course, Quinn." Trevor lifted her body from the couch and carried her to the bedroom, then laid her on the king-size mattress. He kissed up and down her neck, undoing the thin straps across the back of her prom dress. "I'm going to fuck you so hard, Quinn." He ran his fingers over her thighs and under her white panties. "But I think I'm going to kiss you between your legs first, if you have no objection." He pulled the panties down to her ankles, slithering down to her light brown fur and releasing his saliva over her vulva and clitoris. "You know I'm only fucking you for revenge, don't you?" He moved his body over hers and unzipped his tuxedo pants, then effortlessly slid his erection into her unconscious body. "That's okay though. You're only fucking me because I'm famous."

*   *   *

"Wow, Julia—tonight was really fun," Max said, standing in the hallway between their apartments. "I wasn't even planning on going before we met each other, to be honest."

"I had a lot of fun too, Max," Julia said. "Would it be okay if I met your dog really quick? I miss my dog so much."

"He's actually not here right now." Max unlocked his front door. "He's kind of gone with my parents."

"Oh . . ." She smiled. "So where are your parents?"

"I wrote about it in my journal, if you'd want to read it."

"Sure . . . You keep a journal?"

"Only when I feel like something is important enough to write about." Max opened the door. "Are you thirsty or anything, by the way?"

"Do you have any juice?" Julia asked, following him inside.

"Sure, one sec." He walked into the kitchen and returned with a glass.

"Thanks so much. So your diary is in your room?"

"Yeah. I call it a journal though, since Brett says straight guys aren't allowed to keep diaries."

"I see . . ." She followed Max into the bedroom. "Wow, you've got the neatest room of any boy I've ever known."

"Sorry about the mess." Max withdrew the journal from his bookshelf. "Normally the only girl in here is my mom, so I don't really straighten up as much as I should."

"You're kidding, right?" Julia sat on the bed, glancing at the *Abbey Road*-era Beatles poster on the wall. "Where did you get that *poster*, Max? That's so cool."

"At this used record store downtown." Max flipped the journal open to the final entry. "Paul McCartney's cigarette is airbrushed out though, because I guess the poster people thought it sent a bad message to kids or something."

"Weird." She took the journal and read the entry. "Oh my God, Max. That's so *sad*. He actually has cancer?"

"Yeah . . . the closest place that does radiation therapy for dogs is in Colorado. I guess it's kind of silly to spend that kind of money on a pet, but I never had any brothers or sisters or anything so he kind of filled that place for me. I'm really scared."

"We used to have a golden retriever when I was a little kid. She lived to fourteen, which I guess is really old for a dog, but it was just the saddest day of my life when she . . . God, I didn't even come out of my room for two days."

Silence.

"Last year in my biology class there was this one really weird girl." Julia smiled.

"She spent all her free time in the lab and never talked to *anyone,* and the morning her Siamese cat died, she actually brought it into class to *dissect* for her final project."

"Oh my God." Max laughed. "That's insane."

"Even the *teacher* was really creeped out."

"I'm Trevor Fuckin' Thompson. I'm a real cool piece of shit." Brett lay on the bed with his red and white Fender Squire guitar resting against his chest. He picked up the phone and dialed Max's number. "Hey, fucker. How was the shitty prom?"

"Oh, it was really great. Lots of people were there and I even tried dancing."

"So did you fuck her or what? She play a little tune on your flesh flute? Shit, I just got a little bit of that myself from a girl on the Internet who likes her ass slapped raw."

"She's in my bed now and I'm in my parents' because her apartment doesn't have a mattress."

"Jesus Christ, Max." Brett sighed. "Good luck with the whole pitiful faggot thing, all right?" He hung up and dialed Ashley's number. No response came for thirteen rings. "What the fuck, Ash?" He pressed the redial key and waited another fifteen rings.

"—ing . . . please . . . hellllllllllp . . . pilllllls, took the pilllllllssssss . . ."

"Ash?" Brett slammed the phone down and raced outside, then jammed his keys into the Camry's ignition. *"You bastard, you are not out of gas."*

He bolted out of the car and sprinted through the frigid wind until he arrived at Ashley's house seventeen blocks away. He opened the unlocked front door.

"Ash! Ash! Where are you?"

He launched himself up the hardwood staircase and into her empty bedroom, then through the master bedroom, study, guest room and bathroom. Ashley lay naked on the cold linoleum floor, soaked in vomit, reaching upward for the toilet seat.

"Holy God," Brett whispered. "No, Ash, you . . . no, you . . . oh God . . ." He gazed at the plastic orange vials in the sink and the inscription SLUT in red lipstick on the vanity mirror. "Please, God, Ash, you *didn't*." He ran back into the bedroom and dialed 911 on the cellular phone charging on Ashley's oak dresser.

"Emergency?"

"There's, there's a *girl,* and she, oh God, I think she swallowed some pills and she's passed out and I don't know if she's *breathing,* oh God she's not she's not she's—"

"What is your location, sir?"

"It's . . . oh God, it's . . . I don't, I'm not—"

"One moment, I'm going to run a GPS trace on your cellular phone. Keep the victim facedown and monitor her breathing until medical technicians arrive. Do you understand what I'm telling you to do?"

"Yes, God, thank you." Brett ran back to the bathroom and took Ashley's limp frame in his arms. "You stupid fucking girl." He carried her body to the bedroom, fighting back tears. "You stupid, stupid fifteen-year-old girl."

↗ S.L.U.T. STATS

Percentage of sexually active 14-year-old girls who have had intercourse
against their wills: **70**
Percentage of sexually active 15- to 17-year-old girls who have had two or
more sexual partners: **55**
Percentage of sexually active 15- to 17-year-old girls who have had six or
more sexual partners: **13**
[Source: The Alan Guttmacher Institute]

Ratio of American females who will be raped in their lifetimes: **One in three**
[Source: The Federal Bureau of Investigation]

Average age of American female sexual assault victims: **18**
[Source: National Victim Center and Crime Victims Research and Treatment Center]

Number of American females under age 20 who become pregnant each day: **2,800**
[Source: The Alan Guttmacher Institute]

"I don't drink myself, but I don't have anything against having sex with drunk girls. It's like, if she says 'yes' she says 'yes,' and if she's too drunk to say 'no' . . . Well, basically she's saying 'yes.'"

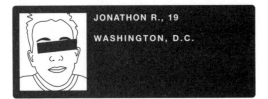

JONATHON R., 19

WASHINGTON, D.C.

"The makers of the bestselling video game <u>Grand Theft Auto</u> are being sued for more than [\$90 million] after two teenagers [aged 14 and 16, from Newport, Tennessee] said they were copying its violent scenes when they killed a man. . . . Points, ammunition and more weapons are awarded [in the game] for completing missions that include stealing cars, shooting pedestrians, drug dealing and beating up prostitutes."
—THE INDEPENDENT [U.K.], SEPTEMBER 18, 2003

↗ S.L.U.T. STATS

70%:
Percentage of American teenage males who have played *Grand Theft Auto*

34%:
Percentage of these who have been in a fist-fight within the last year

30%:
Percentage of American teenage males who have not played *Grand Theft Auto*

17%:
Percentage of these who have been in a fist-fight within the last year
[Source: Reuters, September 16, 2003]

↗ S.L.U.T. STATS

62%:

Percentage of American teenagers who play video games at least one hour per week

25%:

Percentage of American teenagers who play video games at least six hours per week
[Source: Reuters, September 16, 2003]

3rd:

World literacy ranking of Americans educated in the 1950s and '60s

14th:

World literacy ranking of Americans educated in the 1990s
[Source: Educational Testing Service / Stanford University]

18%:

Percentage of American 21-year-olds who have driven under the influence of narcotics
[Source: The Associated Press, September 17, 2003]

"DETROIT—Authorities are investigating whether to press charges
after a 15-year-old patient at University of Michigan C.S. Mott
Children's Hospital sought out an escort service for sex during
his hospital stay this week, according to the Ann Arbor News.
Police believe the teen called an escort service and requested an
escort for Sunday evening. The woman reportedly came to the hospital, where she and the boy engaged in consensual sex—although the
teen is not legally at an age of consent, according to police."
—MSNBC, APRIL 2, 2003

"Last week, when authorities in Brooklyn and Manhattan arrested
10 people on charges of trading child porn online, they clamped
down on the virtual market for young bodies. Counselors and
police say another market, a flesh-and-blood one, also thrives.
Over the last four years, they've noticed an alarming increase
in the number of girls under 18 being pimped on the streets, in
clubs, and through escort services. 'The average age is rapidly
decreasing, so it's not unusual for us to get girls as young as
12 who may have been sexually exploited for a year or two by
that age,' says Rachel Lloyd, director of the Manhattan-based
Girls Educational and Mentoring Services (GEMS). No one knows
exactly how many girls in New York are pressed into sex work..."
—THE VILLAGE VOICE, JULY 17, 2002

"'Potentially good sex is a small price to pay for the freedom
to spend money on what I want,' says 17-year-old Stacey, who
liked to hang out after school at the Mall of America,
Minnesota's vast shopping megaplex. After being approached last
summer by a man who told her how pretty she was, and asked if
he could buy her some clothes, Stacey agreed and went home
that night with a $250 outfit. Stacey, who lives with her par-
ents in an upscale neighborhood, began stripping for men in
hotel rooms—then went on to more intimate activities. She
placed ads on a local telephone personals service, offering
'wealthy, generous' men 'an evening of fun' for $400."
—NEWSWEEK, AUGUST 10, 2003

MY UNFORGETTABLE [ALMOST] PROM DATE WITH A DIRTY ROTTEN WHORE

A Tale of Hope, A Saga of Redemption

"For older teens [in the 1950s] the prom remained the most public, most ritualized dating event—also often the most expensive.... As part of their symbolic entry into the adult world at graduation, teens dressed in more adult formal clothes, listened to more adult music, wore orchids as symbols of sexual maturity, and generally behaved with adult decorum—at least publicly. The competition for a prom date was also intense, and the lack of a date was a visible failure."

—FROM TWENTIETH-CENTURY TEEN CULTURE BY THE DECADES: A REFERENCE GUIDE BY LUCY ROLLIN, GREENWOOD PRESS, 1999

"For true and righteous are HIS judgments; for He hath judged the great Whore, which did corrupt the earth with her fornication, and hath avenged the blood of HIS servants at her hand."

—REVELATION 19:2

Monday, December 4, 2000

Approximately 6:30 p.m.

"So the prom is Saturday night?" Mommy asks from across the dinner table.

"Guess so," I say, taking a hearty bite of my peanut butter and jelly sandwich, and then washing it down with the hearty glass of gin and orange juice my mother believes to be merely the latter. Ha! Ha! I need help!

"Don't you have a date?" Mommy asks.

"Nope," I say. "Not going."

"I think you'd have a *fun* time if you went, Marty. You need to get out of the house more often. Now, which girl can you take?"

"Not *going*, Mom."

"How about your friend Jessica? She'd go with you, wouldn't she?"

"Not *going.*"

"Or that girl whose mother I work with? Lizzie, is that her name?"

"Mom, I'm not *go—*"

"Or how about Melissa? Isn't she nice? *She's* nice, isn't she?"

"Mom!" I scream. "I don't *want* to go to the stupid pr—uh . . . hmm. . . . Well, now that you mention it, I guess I do have one idea."

"Oh, good," Mommy says with visible relief. "Who?"

"A dirty, filthy *prostitute,* Mommy!"

"You were such a cute child," Mommy sighs. "You know that, don't you? Such a *nice* child."

"I won't have *sex* with the prostitute, Mom. I'll just take her to dinner, dance with her a little . . . You know, show her a good time."

"Why don't you take one of your *friends* to prom, Marty? That would be *nice,* wouldn't it? One of your *friends?*"

"Well, see, I *would,* Mom. I really would, but none of my friends are dirty, filthy prostitutes and I'm getting pretty darn set on taking a dirty, filthy prostitute to prom. So I guess I'll just have to go ahead and hunt me down a dirty, filthy prostitute before—"

"Fine!" Mommy bangs her fists against the table. "You just *go ahead* and *do* what *you want.* Will that make you *happy,* getting *your* way? Will it? *Will* that make you *happy?"*

"Hello!" Dad suddenly walks through the front door with his briefcase after a long day at the office.

"Your *son* has a *question* for you," Mommy says. "Why don't you *listen* to your son's *question?"*

"Yes?" Dad asks. "What is it, son?"

"Well, Dad, I want to take a hooker to prom. I already told Mom that I wouldn't have sex with her or anything—I mean the hooker, not Mom, um, obviously—but I'll take her to dinner and show her off to all my buddies and we'll all have a good laugh over it and . . . um . . . well, stuff. You know?"

(Long, awkward silence.)

"Go for it," Dad chuckles.

"It's not *safe* to deal with *shady characters!*" Mommy wails. "Marty, you don't *know* these people. They could be *dangerous.* How do you know they won't *shoot* you? Are you *listening* to me? You don't know what you're getting *into,* Martin Seth Beckerman. You have *no idea* what you're getting yourself *into.*"

"Um, Mom?" I ask. "You're not going to cry now, are you?"

"escort \ n: one (as a person or warship) accompanying another esp. as a protection or courtesy."

—THE NEW MERRIAM-WEBSTER DICTIONARY

"Exquisite Taste Dating Escort Service
- 24-hour Service
- In and Out Calls
- Private Parties
- Bachelor Parties
- Female and Male Escorts
- Couples
- Tourists and Conventioneers Discount

Most Elegant and Tantalizing Ladies/Men in Alaska: 569-YUMM"

—ADVERTISEMENT FROM THE ACS ANCHORAGE/MAT-SU VALLEY YELLOW PAGES, ALASKA COMMUNICATIONS SYSTEMS, 1999

Tuesday, December 5, 2000

Approximately 10:45 p.m.

"Exquisite Taste," the candy-voiced girl answers the telephone. "This is Julie."

"Hi there, Julie," I say, already feeling like an uncanny pervert. "This is five-six-nine YUMM?"

"Yes. What can we do for you?"

"Well, Julie, I'm looking for a prom date for Saturday night, and all I'm interested in is dinner and dancing, nothing else. I mean, not that I could actually *pay* for anything else, because, well, see, that would be *illegal* and I'm sure an upstanding establishment such as yours would never—"

"That's fine, hon. But we *do* charge a fee of two hundred and fifty dollars for the hour. Is that all right?"

"Two hundred and fifty for one hour?"

"Yes, but it's absolutely *worth* it because the girls who work for me are *gorgeous*. Trust me, it's *not* a waste of your money. My girls are *ten* times better than anyone else you could *possibly* have for a prom date."

"Yeah, sure, but . . . Good Lord, *two hundred and fifty?*"

"That's what it costs, hon. Take it or leave it."

"Hey, Dad?" I yell upstairs. "Can I have two hundred and fifty bucks?"

"Try finding a *cheap* whore first," Dad hollers back. "That's your best bet."

"All right," I acquiesce. "Hey, Julie? Um, sorry, I don't think it's going to . . . Julie? Hello? Hey, Julie? Hello? Um, Julie?"

Now, it must be noted before we go any further that there technically is a difference between escort services and brothels, and this distinction allows the former to be legal (and licensed) nationwide while the latter are banned nearly everywhere in America. You see, it's all due to a widely enacted legal loophole that allows escorts to be paid solely for their Time and Company, therefore rendering it the escort's *choice* whether to partake in sexual acts with her (always willing) clients. Subsequently, this reporter isn't at all suggesting that the job of any escort from any escort service anywhere is to actually escort men into her Dirty Rotten Escort Pussy, as that would be inaccurate and most likely libelous. (And true.)

Saturday, December 9, 2000
(Prom Night)

Approximately 7:30 p.m.

So after four days of laborious searching and price haggling, I finally manage to find a willing and affordable prom date from one of Anchorage's total *fifty-two* licensed escort services.[1] Although the actual *name* of the escort and her place of employment obviously can't be revealed here, each will instead be given an adequate and incredibly juvenile pseudonym: Henceforth, the escort service in question shall be referred to as "Super Snatch Mart U.S.A." and my date for the evening, "Octopussy."

"*Ohhhhhhhh,*" Mommy chirps, as I emerge from my bedroom in a loose-fitting brown suit and matching hazel tie. "You know, Marty, it's not too late to change your mind about the prostitute. You can just go by *yourself,* can't you? There's nothing wrong with going by *yourself,* is there?"

"Oh God, Mom," I sigh, opening the front door. "I'll see you later tonight, I promise. And if I'm not home by curfew, just check the river. I'll be the cold, dead body floating facedown towards the ocean."

"*My baby,*" Mommy howls, rushing down the stairs for one last embrace. "Oh, my *baby.*"

"Don't *touch* me!" I command, breaking away from my frail mother's grasp and racing outside to my 1984 Dodge MiniVan, speeding off moments later into the frigid

---

1 / Insert your own "something has to keep those crazy Eskimos warm all winter" joke here.

Alaskan night.
Approximately 7:50 p.m.

The Avenue isn't exactly what you might call a *pleasant* location after dark,
unless of course you happen to find pleasure in drunken and/or drugged vagrants,
barbwire fencing, broken automobiles and seedy escort services with names such
as the Fantasy Club, the Moon House and the Alaska Trap Line. However, putting
aside my own cowardly fear of this bleak and rotten place, I presently approach
the entrance of Super Snatch Mart U.S.A. and walk inside, soon finding myself in
a narrow hallway bordered by rusty chains and leading to an ominous black steel
door.

Give me strength, Lord, I plead, breathing heavily. *Christ, Jesus . . . Oh God, I
want my Mommy. I'm so sorry, Mommy. I'm so, so sorry and I love you and I'll
never be able to tell you that now and I don't want to die, God, I'm only seventeen
years old and I don't know anything and I don't want to die, I don't want to die, I
don't want to—*

"Hello," says the shriveled, eighty-year-old Asian lady presently standing in the doorway. "You open eyes now?"

"Oh, *shit.*" I exhale, wiping a gallon of cold sweat off my forehead. "Hi, I called about
taking a girl to my high school prom?"

"Ah, yes," the old lady says, leading me through the doorway into a room consider-
ably more homely than the wretched antechamber: Fluffy pink couches abound, large
patterned mirrors cover the walls and dozens of thick red candles are lit everywhere.
On top of all that, Octopussy stands in the middle of the room, licking what appears to
be dark chocolate off her fingertips.

"Wow," I say, taking in the cozy bordello atmosphere.

"Do you like?" the old lady asks, pointing to her employee, an Asian girl in her late
twenties wearing heavy red lipstick and a slinky minidress with its own cut-out cleavage window.

"Hi," I say to Octopussy.

"Hi." Octopussy smiles.

"Where you take girl tonight?" the old lady asks, humorously attempting to speak Holy White Man's English.

"Well," I say, "dinner, first of all."

"Ah, yes, where you take girl dinner?"

"I was actually thinking McDonald's,[2] if that works for you."

"What?" Octopussy yaps. *"You're paying a hundred and fifty dollars to take me to McDonald's?"*

"Well, you seem like a classy girl, and I figure what the hell—a classy girl deserves a classy meal, right? Shall we be on our way?"[2]

"I call cab!" The old lady briskly toddles back to her office.

"You've never been to a place like this before, have you?" Octopussy sits on one of the pink couches and lights a Camel cigarette.

"Not really." I sit on the couch and take a cigarette from Octopussy's pack of thirty. "I don't even know the difference between in calls and out calls, if you want to know the truth."

"Oh, it's easy." She lights my cigarette. "With out calls we go someplace with someone, and with in calls we just stay here and go into the back."

"Okay . . . So, like, how'd you get into the business?"

"I was eighteen when I got started. I don't know, I had a friend who was into it and she was making like a thousand a night so I just—"

"Whoa!" I shout. *"Holy shit."*

"Yeah." Octopussy laughs. "The money was good and my friend got me connected with some people in Seattle. I don't know . . . Most girls do this because they were abused as kids or got into drugs in high school or whatever, but I just really, really like the money."

"That's cool . . . I mean, whatever makes you happy, right?"

"Something like that." Octopussy takes a long drag off her cigarette.

---

2 / In the extremely unlikely case this volume is read by future generations such as Homer's Odyssey and the Bible are read today, it should be noted that, in the year 2003 a.d., McDonald's, Inc. is by far the largest restaurant chain on the planet, with more than thirty thousand locations in 121 countries. According to Fast Food Nation: The Dark Side of the All-American Meal by Eric Schlosser (Houghton Mifflin, 2000), more (con't)

"Cab here," the old lady says, returning from her office. "You pay now?"

"Fair enough." I draw one hundred and fifty dollars from my wallet and give it to the withered female immigrant. Octopussy leads me into an orange, checkered taxi outside, and we soon arrive at the McDonald's on Arctic Boulevard. As always, the aroma of fried, morbidly unhealthful fast food permeates the air like a fine perfume, only cheaper.

"Welcome to McDonald's," says the sullen adolescent employee behind the cash register. "How may I take your order?"

"What would you like, darling?" I ask Octopussy.

"I'll just have a four-piece Chicken McNugget meal," she says. "I'm not too hungry right now."

"One four-piece Chicken McNugget meal for the McLady," I repeat to the McSubordinate. "And I'll have the McSame, thank you."

"Why are you paying to take me to McDonald's?" Octopussy asks after we receive our McNuggets and french fries.

"That's not important right now," I say. "What's important is that I have a secret to tell you."

"Okay . . ." Octopussy says. "What?"

"My parents are here. I'd like you to meet them."

(Long, awkward silence.)

"You're joking," Octopussy says.

"Nope." I point to the table at which my mother and father presently sit. "They're right over there."

"You . . . you set this up . . . ?"

"Pretty much," I say, leading her across the restaurant. "Mom and Dad, this is my date, [Ms. Pussy]. Darling, these are my parents."

"Ah, yes, it's good to see our son out with a nice girl like you," Dad says. "We were concerned for some time that Marty was a homosexual, but now we know for sure that he's straight as an arrow. Praise Allah."

than 90 percent of American children enjoy at least one greasy, disgusting McDonald's meal each month, and the average American adult "dines" there between three and four times a week. It is easily the least classy restaurant in the History of Man.

"Oh . . ." Octopussy gulps.

"Hi," Mommy says, visibly relieved that I'm not dead.

"Have some food," I say, gesturing toward the tray of greasy (yet so delicious) McSwill. Octopussy timidly bites into a couple fries.

"I've seen enough," Mommy says. "We're making the poor girl nervous."

"Well," Dad stands and puts on his jacket, "it was good meeting you. Have fun at our son's prom."

"Okay," Octopussy says, still dazed. "Thank you?"

"So . . ." I say after my parents have left the premises. "How long do you think you'll stay an escort and everything?"

"Oh, I was in a car wreck in Seattle—I had to get stitches in my hand and metal rods in my back—so I had some medical bills to pay off. But that's pretty much taken care of now. I want to start my own business someday."

"Your own escort service?" I ask.

"Yeah, I'll have girls working for me."

"You know, it's good to have a dream."

Octopussy nods her head in agreement.

"So I bet you get a bunch of rich middle-aged doctors and lawyers coming in to cheat on their wives and stuff, huh?"

"Oh *God*." She groans. "All the *time*."

Our McNugget dinners fully devoured at this point, Octopussy withdraws a cellular phone from her red purse and calls the taxi dispatcher for a ride to the prom.

"Don't you think the price is kind of steep?" I ask after she hangs up. "I mean, I don't want to sound like a Cheap Shylock or anything, but do you really think what you do is *worth* a hundred and fifty bucks an hour?"

"What is *that* question supposed to mean?"

"Do you really think one-fifty is a reasonable price?"

"Back in Seattle the standard was *two*-fifty. I have a friend in San Francisco who makes *four hundred* per hour. What I get here is *nothing*."

"I guess I got a good deal then." I take a bite of my last remaining french fry. The next twenty-five minutes pass in silence. The taxi still hasn't arrived.

"Wait," Octopussy says. "This isn't the McDonald's on *Arctic,* is it?"

"Yeah," I say. "So?"

"Shit, I told the cab to pick us up at the one down*town.*"

"Oh, good *job,*" I sneer, immediately understanding the implications of this royal fuck-up: My hour with Octopussy is nearly over, and if she's still to be my prom date, I'll need to pay her *another* hundred and fifty dollars for the privilege.

"It was an accident," she says before telephoning the dispatcher again. Ten minutes later a taxi arrives and returns us to the street side entrance of Super Snatch Mart U.S.A., where we say our curt good-byes. She disappears into the escort service and I walk back to my 1984 Dodge MiniVan, disappointed in the night's events to say the least.

Until, that is, I find the white corsage I purchased earlier lying on the MiniVan's passenger seat, giving me an unbearably emotional reminder of what tonight could have been had things gone differently. Overcome with shame and regret, I find myself knocking again upon Super Snatch Mart U.S.A.'s black steel door.

"Yes?" asks the old lady, clearly surprised to see me.

"I have a present for my date," I explain, presenting the flower wristband.

"*Ohhhhhhhhhhhhhhhhhhh,*" the old lady squeals. "You come *in!* You come *in!*"

I follow her into the pink and red lounge, where Octopussy is flirting with her next customer, a dirty bearded man at least three times my age.

"Hey, I forgot to give this to you," I say, presenting the corsage.

"*Ohhhhhhhhhhhhhhhhhh,*" Octopussy moans, holding out her hand.

"You come back again?" the old lady asks.

"Um," I say. "No."

"*Ohhhhhhhhhhhhhhhhhh,*" the old lady moans. "Why you not come back?"

"Sorry." I turn away. "It was just a one-time thing."

"*Ohhhhhhhhhhhhhhhhhh,*" the old lady moans.

"Ohhhhhhhhhhhhhhhhh," Octopussy moans.

"Ohhhhhhhhhhhhhhhh," the old lady moans.

"Ohhhhhhhhhhhhhhhhh," Octopussy moans.

"Ohhhhhhhhhhhhhhhhh," the old lady moans.

"Ohhhhhhhhhhhhhhhhh," Octopussy moans.

Fucking whores.

"Alcohol gives you an excuse that next day after it happens. If you hook up with a really ugly guy or something, you can just say you were drunk and it's not a big deal. Like, take my first time: I was really, really drunk and I didn't know what was going on and the guy was just like, 'Take off your pants.' And it was really bad; he had a really small dick. I mean I couldn't even feel it!"

LISA C., 16

FARGO, NORTH DAKOTA

"I was down in this girl's dorm room last night, and she was complaining about how there aren't enough guys at this school. So I told her I've been having trouble finding girls too and maybe we should go out sometime, but she said she doesn't ever date short guys. Then she told me if I had anything to drink up in my room, she might let me take her shirt off."

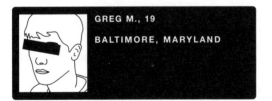

GREG M., 19

BALTIMORE, MARYLAND

"Six months pregnant, 16-year-old Tinesha Bost of Charlotte, N.C., told her mother she was going to the grocery store one evening in February 2000 and never returned. Police found her body floating facedown in a nearby pond later that night. She'd been shot and dumped there by her boyfriend, who apparently thought having another kid would be a drag."
—JANE MAGAZINE, APRIL 2003

JAKE K., 15

PROVIDENCE, RHODE ISLAND

"At our spring dance last year some girl asked me to dance with her, then she unbuttoned her jeans on the dance floor and put my hand down her pants. I got two fingers in, so I guess that means she liked it."

JESSICA A., 19

PORTLAND, OREGON

"A lot of girls feel uncomfortable being in control of their sexuality, but if I want to be in a relationship I will and if I want to get laid I will. And if I want to get so drunk I can't remember what the hell I did last night, I will."

SUNDAY

↗ SUNDAY

"Oh . . . so I'm going to be okay?"

"Your vital signs are fine." The Doctor withdrew a Xeroxed document from the over-flowing manila folder. "There is the issue of sustained treatment, however. May I sug-gest a temporary change of environment, Miss Iverson? Perhaps a place where you could speak about what's been on your mind of late?"

"What do you mean? Why would I want to change my *environment?*"

"Your signature is needed to confirm your entrance into Inpatient Services." The Doctor handed Ashley the document and a felt-tip pen. "I'll be able to perform an ini-tial evaluation by the end of the day. Your room will be prepared by nightfall."

"Evaluation? What evaluation? I don't understand what you *mean.*"

"Inpatient Services are administered in three-week to fifteen-month programs, Miss Iverson. Typically the comprehensive evaluation process takes three to five days, at which point a recommendation will be made for the best treatment option in your individual case."

"And I'm sorry, if I *don't* sign the contract you're holding?"

"It's not a *contract,* Miss Iverson, simply a custodial release charging the hospital with your care. As soon as our doctors determine that your treatment has been suc-cessfully completed, you're free to go."

"Okay, but shouldn't . . . I mean, shouldn't I talk to my parents or something before signing any kind of—"

"Should the custodial release fail to be signed at the time of your discharge from the

Emergency Ward, Grace Alliance Medical Center is required by law to submit your records to the State Department of Child and Family Services. Are you aware that attempted suicide is a *legal offense,* Miss Iverson?"

"Listen, I don't *need* this, all right? I just felt weird last night because it was prom and nobody *invited* me and I just. . . . Don't you *understand?* I'm not fucking *crazy.*"

"Our Youth Ward has an unparalleled reputation in adolescent rehabilitation, Miss Iverson." The Doctor motioned toward the release form. "The business office has already approved your parents' insurance to cover the one-thousand-dollar daily expense. You have every reason to consider yourself fortunate."

"Good fucking job, Maxwell." Brett walked through the apartment doorway, carrying his skateboard and chewing on an unlit cigarette. "You probably pushed her to it."

"Pushed who to what?" Max rubbed his eyes. "What *time* is it?"

"One-thirty. You must've gotten real tired not fucking your girlfriend last night."

"She's not my *girlfriend,* Brett . . . She's not still *here,* is she?"

"Like I know. Oh, by the way, Ashley tried to kill herself last night."

"Wait . . . you . . . you mean *Ashley* Ashley? Like, Ashley-who-didn't-remember-my-*name* Ashley? How did *I* push her to it? You had sex with her too, didn't you?"

"Yeah, like five *months* ago. She didn't try to *kill* herself *then.*"

"Tell me you're making this up, Brett. Please tell me you're not being serious."

"The emergency room guys told me she would've *died* if I hadn't found her on the bathroom floor. And Christ, I was only seeing if she wanted any thick white cock on prom night. I mean, what the fuck, right?"

"So what happens now? Is she still in the hospital or going home or—?"

"The doctors said she'd be fine. She'll probably be committed to some kind of psycho fuck-up ward for a few weeks though. Or years. Or whatever."

"Oh my God, Brett. You don't really think it has anything to do with me, do you? You don't really think I had something to do with why she wanted to kill herself?"

"Naaah, don't worry about it, dude. Hey, you want to go get a milkshake at McDonald's? It'll make you feel better about driving Ashley to suicide and everything."

"I . . . I should probably work on this *Brave New World* speech for Ms. Lovelace. It's twenty percent of our grade and all, so I should probably just stay and work on that."

"We've got an oral exam for *Lovelace* tomorrow?"

"You have to pick a book from the last hundred years and relate it to Shakespeare. Remember?"

"Whatever, dude." Brett smirked. "Lovelace can't touch me."

"What are you talking about? She's not going to fail you just because you're the track champion or something?"

"No, Maxwell, teachers don't actually do that. Lovelace can't touch me because she *already* touched me. Bitch gave me an extra-special kind of oral exam on a personal field trip to the Holiday Inn."

"Okay, Brett, sure, whatever." Max laughed. "I'll believe some of the stuff you say, but not crazy stuff like having sex with our teacher."

"She kept crying afterward about how she could lose her job and go to jail, but I'm just such a beautiful boy and blah blah blah blah blah blah. Good Christ, I actually had to like *hold* her and shit."

"You're so full of it, Brett. I mean, you would've told me or bragged about it to someone at least. You're totally making this up."

"Dude, do you *think* I tell you about all the girls I hook up with? Fuck, I wouldn't want to make you all jealous and shit, would I? And besides, I felt kind of guilty about the whole thing afterward. I mean, Christ, she's like our fucking teacher, you know?"

"Oh God, Brett. How can we even talk like this when Ashley just tried to kill herself?"

"Ashley's going to be fine, don't worry about that little fucking whore. I'm visiting her in the hospital tomorrow. I'll let you know what I find out."

"Could you just tell her I'm really sorry for making her try to kill herself? Because I never would've wanted that and I wish I could change everything and never go to that stupid party or get drunk or—"

"Please, Maxwell. It's not your fault this girl is an insane melodramatic cunt, all right? A guilty conscience will get you nowhere in life, and don't you forget that."

Brett closed the door and pressed the elevator call button in the hallway, then stepped forward just as—

"I'm his friend Brett. Maybe he's mentioned me?"

"Oh, you're the one who hates the Beatles, right?"

"Hates the *Beatles?* 'Homeward Bound' is a *great* song."

"Um . . . 'Homeward Bound' is by Paul Simon actually."

"Well, yeah. And Paul Simon wasn't in the Beatles?"

"No." Julia laughed. "Paul *McCartney* was in the Beatles."

"Oh, right. Well, I guess you called my bullshit, huh?"

"That's okay . . . So how long have you been skateboarding?"

"Like four or five years now. This is actually a *long board* though. You can't do tricks on it, but you go so amazingly fast down hills or into traffic or whatever. Anyway, the snow melted this morning so I just figured I'd drive over to this hill near my house and try to kill myself. You want to give it a shot?"

"I don't know. . . . I'm not very coordinated sometimes. Or ever."

"Come on, Jules. You haven't lived yet."

"No, no, nope, not a good idea. Thanks anyway."

"Come on, I promise you won't regret it. Swear to God."

"Well . . . okay, maybe I'll try it *once*. But if I accidentally break my neck or anything, it's your fault."

"Awesome." Brett smirked. "You're going to be such a skater girl."

"One sec, I need to drop off these books first." She unlocked her front door and walked inside. "Feel free to come in. There's not too much to see, I guess."

"Wow, I like the boxes." Brett scanned the unfurnished room. "Nice look for you. Very modern. Very boxish."

"I'm still unpacking." Julia blushed. "Actually I had to sleep in Max's bed last night . . . I mean, we didn't sleep *together* or anything."

"Of course not." Brett fingered the condom in his pocket as Julia walked down the hallway. "So where are your parents?"

"Oh, they're still in Anchorage. I'm . . . I'm kind of trying to live by myself for a while. You know, the whole emancipation thing."

"Anchorage? Holy shit . . . So what do you have in the bag?"

"Oh, I bought *A Separate Peace* and *Ender's Game* because I haven't read them and everyone says they're really good, and a copy of *The Perks of Being a Wallflower* for Max because it's my favorite book and I think he'd really like it. Actually it's the first book that ever made me cry . . . What's the best thing you've ever read, Brett?"

"Well, have you ever heard of *Super Asian Gang Bang Monthly?* No, wait, just kidding. . . . So what's this *Wallflower* book of yours about?"

"It's about this kid named Charlie—I think he's fourteen or fifteen—and he doesn't have any control over his emotions, so he goes through all these situations that I think a lot of kids do growing up, and you see how someone who can't stop crying reacts to things that most people deal with by walling themselves off. It's actually published by MTV Books, and personally I think MTV is kind of everything that's wrong with America to be honest, but the book's still really, really good."

"MTV *Books?"* Brett groaned, covering his face with both hands. "My God, the world is going to fucking hell."

"Of course, you'll be on one-to-one watch for the first twenty-four hours," the Doctor said, leading Ashley through the corridors of the Grace Alliance Youth Ward. "Typically, incoming patients' clothes are returned within three days, shoes within five."

"You mean I have to wear these *pajamas* for *three days?"*

"Apologies. It's all to prevent flight impulse."

"Flight impulse? What's *flight* impulse?"

"As you can imagine, many of our incoming patients hold a strong dislike for clinical treatment. Some even attempt escaping, which becomes difficult without clothes or shoes."

Ashley glanced over the multicolored posters hanging on the corridor walls: NOTHING WAS EVER ACCOMPLISHED WITHOUT ENTHUSIASM! and YOU CAN DO ANYTHING YOU SET YOUR MIND TO!

"You'll soon discover, Miss Iverson, that this facility maintains a system of rewarding good behavior and punishing noncompliance. Good behavior leads to increased freedoms. Hopefully we need not discuss the consequences of noncompliance."

"What are all these rooms for?" Ashley asked, looking down the corridor.

"To our left are the faculty-oriented components of the ward—doctors' offices, meeting rooms, staff lounge and nurses' stations. To the right are patient domiciles, cafeteria, TV lounge, showers and common restrooms. Also the monitored Hygiene Room for shaving and handling authorized sharps."

"We don't have our own *bathrooms?* That's so *gross.*"

"If you think that's awful, Miss Iverson, just wait until you get to college."

At the far end of the corridor a nurse led three emaciated girls—their forearms and wrists all bandaged—into the Hygiene Room.

"Did those girls cut themselves or something?" Ashley asked. "Before they came here?"

"Most of the patients in this ward are self-mutilators, Miss Iverson. Sexual abuse and family neglect are generally to blame, but other factors can contribute as well. It's estimated that two million Americans have the disorder."

"That's really disgusting. I mean, God, that's like *hacking yourself up* and stuff. How could anyone actually *do* that to themselves?"

"That's an excellent question, Miss Iverson. You'll have an opportunity to discuss it with your fellow patients tomorrow in Group Therapy."

The Doctor unlocked the door to one of the patient bedrooms.

"—*oh God, oh God, baby, fuck me, fuck me, fuck my pussy, fuck my motherfucking pussy.*" The emaciated girl lay spread on the mattress, underneath a lanky adolescent marred with peeling flesh.

"This is the last time you two get away with this." The Doctor grabbed the pock-marked boy's left arm and tugged him off the mattress. "You're going back to Solitary. Effective immediately."

"*I'm . . . I'm . . . Oh God, I'm coming,*" the boy moaned, oblivious to the Doctor, whose suit jacket he presently ejaculated upon. "*Oh . . . oh God, oh God, I'm coming, baby, I'm . . . I'm . . . unnnnnnnnnnnnnhhhhhh.*"

"*Zero privileges,*" the Doctor screamed. "*Solitary, Solitary, Solitary.*" He dragged the twitching young man through the doorway and down the hospital corridor.

"Sorry for the flesh show and everything." The girl sat up and slipped on a pair of aquamarine panties. "The nurse wasn't supposed to come around on checks for five minutes. . . . First impressions always suck anyway, right?"

"You're . . . You're going to be my roommate or something?" Ashley asked. "I mean . . . um . . . Hi, I'm Ashley."

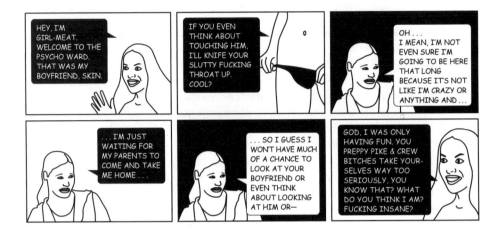

"I . . . I don't think I like it here very much." Ashley adjusted the striped pajama bottoms. "The doctor said I don't get my clothes back until Wednesday and these pants keep falling down and it's really *annoying* and oh God I just want to go *home*."

"Pants keep falling down? Is that the reason you're here in the first place, or did Pike & *Cunt* just run out of fucking khakis this weekend?"

The trio of bandaged girls and the nurse passed outside the bedroom.

"Oh my God," Ashley said. "They look like *zombies* or something."

"When one starts cutting again, all the rest follow." Girl-Meat pulled a tattered NOFX T-shirt over her chest and looked out the barred window. "It's the only thing about this place that still freaks me out to be honest, except for all the force-feedings and electroshocks and stuff. But you get used to that shit after a while, you know?"

"And you *promise* I'll be okay?" Julia stood with one foot on the wooden skateboard deck and the other planted on the black pavement. She looked with pounding fear down the steep hill, bordered on each side by two-story homes.

"Of *course* you'll be okay." Brett placed a hand on her shoulder. "Just try not to kill yourself before you reach the bottom, all right?"

"That's not *funny*, Brett."

"Sorry. You'll do fine."

"Okay . . . if you really think I'll be all right . . ."

She placed her grounded foot on the wooden deck. The plastic wheels spun beneath her.

"Oh God!" She leapt off the skateboard before rolling three feet downhill.

"Come *on,* Jules. You can do better than *that."*

"I was *scared.* I don't *like* it when I'm *scared."*

"What about if I run down right beside you? If you fall off or get hit by a giant truck or something, I'll be right there to catch and/or cradle you. All right?"

"Well . . . okay . . ." She stepped back onto the skateboard. "But I don't want to get hit by a giant truck."

The wheels spun.

"I'm doing it!"

"You're doing it!"

"I'm doing it!"

"You're doing it!"

"I'm doing it!"

"You're going to crash!"

"What?" She looked up at the eight-foot-wide steel Dumpster at the bottom of the hill. *"Eeeeek! Brett! Help!"*

"Hold on." He wrapped his arms around her waist and flung their bodies to the sidewalk, landing on his back to cushion her fall. The skateboard rebounded six feet into the air and shattered upturned on the pavement.

"Oh God," she whimpered. "Oh God oh God oh God oh God oh—"

"We're okay, Jules," Brett laughed, tightening his grip. "We're going to *live."*

"The main theme of *Brave New World* is that happiness doesn't always equal freedom, and sometimes it even equals slavery," Max scribbled on the three-by-five-inch note-card. He scratched over the text and wrote instead *Max ♥s Julia.*

A knock came at the front door. Max walked across the apartment.

"Hey there, little buddy." Trevor stood in the doorway, wearing a Pike & Crew over-shirt and crimson Oakley sunglasses. "How's it going?"

"Trevor Thompson? How—? Why—?"

"Quinn told me where you live between GHB feedings, so I thought I'd fire up the BMW and pay you a visit." Trevor invited himself into the apartment and closed the door. "Listen, Max, you want to come to this killer party I'm having at my apartment Tuesday night? Girls with boyfriends wear red, girls who could go either way wear yellow, and girls who want to get fucked for sure wear green. Your odds are beyond optimal."

"Um . . . I . . . I . . . Wait, *how* do you know who I am?"

"You *are* Brett Hunter's best friend, aren't you?"

"Well, yeah, I guess so. You know Brett?"

"We've fucked around town a couple times." Trevor placed a hand on Max's shoulder. "Listen, Max, you don't smoke by any chance, do you?"

"Cigarettes? Not really. Why?"

"Not *cigarettes,* man. *Chronic.*"

"So that's like marijuana? Because I don't smoke that either."

"That's cool. I was just headed out to the Point to light up myself. If you want to come along, you're more than welcome. No pressure to smoke."

"Oh, I was just working on a speech for English tomorrow, but I guess I could take a break for a while."

"You're taking Lovelace, aren't you?"

"Oh yeah, it's just about my favorite class . . . So you still have to take English even though you're a published author?"

"Need the credit to graduate." Trevor fondled the marijuana pipe in his pants pocket. "Not that I actually *need* a high school diploma, considering I've already amassed a fortune for your average eighteen-year-old, but my agent insists on keeping some asinine All-American teenager image. Which apparently entails finishing through my senior year."

"So I guess if you know Brett that well, you probably know he's basically in love with Quinn, right?"

"If you're suggesting I should feel guilty that his ex-girlfriend only likes him as a friend now, Max, you're on shaky fucking ground." Trevor opened the front door and stepped into the hallway. "All's fair in love and whores."

"He's pretty upset by the whole thing. Maybe you guys aren't that close, but I don't think I could ever do that to a friend, and I don't think Brett would ever do that to me either."

"Max, Max, Max." Trevor shook his head. "Have you ever considered how *blind* you are thanks to your friendship with him? You *do* know he got Ashley Iverson *pregnant* five months ago, don't you? You *do* know he abandoned her at the abortion clinic, *don't* you?"

"Allow me to explain borderline personality disorder, Miss Iverson." The Doctor crossed his legs in the burgundy leather chair. "It's too early to make a concrete diagnosis, of course, but borderline personality is one of the more common disorders with our female patients."

"Okay . . ." Ashley squirmed on the leather couch. "I don't think anything's wrong with my personality though."

"Having a disorder doesn't mean something is 'wrong' with you. All it means is that an individual must take certain precautions to assimilate within society and lead a fulfilling life. Borderline personality disorder means an individual is unstable in his or her self-perception, often leading to difficulty maintaining stable, long-term relationships. On the other hand, *histrionic* personality disorder means the individual is obsessively self-conscious, behaving dramatically in inappropriate situations and compulsively seeking validation from others. Combine these with *dependent* personality disorder—desperate lack of self-confidence—and I'd say you have an accurate profile of the typical adolescent female. Wouldn't you agree, Miss Iverson?"

"You have *no idea* what it's like," Ashley snapped.

"Apologies. Why don't you tell me what it's like?"

"You . . . you have to smile when you're not happy, and every guy you meet only wants one thing from you even if they don't say anything." She looked down at the floor. "And you have to make them *think* they can get you because that's why they talk to you in the first place, and you *want* them to talk to you because they're *boys* and you *like them* and that's just *natural,* right? And you spend all day in front of mirrors trying to look perfect so they'll like you, and then they make their move at a party or whatever and it's like you don't even have a *choice* anymore because you just want them to *like* you even though it's so obvious they only want to get in your pants, but you let them anyway because you just want someone to . . . God, why am I even *telling* you this?"

The Doctor wrote briskly in his leather notebook. "You've engaged in sexual intercourse?"

"Well, God, I'm *in* ninth grade." Ashley rolled her eyes. "Sorry, I didn't mean that to sound all bitchy. . . . Um, I kind of got pregnant one time too, but I got an abortion and stuff so nothing really happened with that or anything."

"Very interesting. Would you care to tell me about the boy who contributed?"

"Oh . . . I . . . I'm not really sure about that." Ashley closed her eyes. "I'm not really sure which one it was actually."

"I'm a little scared of moving to a new place, to be honest." Julia sat in the passenger seat of Brett's Camry as he drove outside the city limits. "Actually I think I'm a lot scared of moving to a new place."

"You'll get used to this town before you know it." He placed the Bad Religion album *Against the Grain* into the dashboard stereo. "When I was a little kid I used to sleep upstairs in the room right next to my parents' and brother's, right? But when I was like ten or eleven, I went to summer camp for a few weeks. When I came home, they'd moved everything I owned downstairs. Apparently my dad wanted his office upstairs and thought it would be a nice surprise to rape my childhood and everything. I wouldn't sleep in my new bedroom for like six whole months." He steered the car onto the side of the road, next to a wooded area. "And every night I'd take my pillow and blanket upstairs and sleep on the floor of my old room, until I finally came to the realization that it's kind of cool having the whole downstairs to myself, you know? It was just a blessing in disguise."

"Maybe being here is a blessing in disguise too." Julia looked out the window. "Or maybe meeting you and Max is the real bless—"

"What the *fuck?*" Brett shouted as Trevor's BMW came speeding in the opposite direction. "Was *Maxwell* in that car? Smoking a *bong?*"

"I don't know, I was looking out the other window. What's a bong?"

"Never should've downed those fucking shrooms last summer, I'm *still* hallucinating." Brett unbuckled his seat belt and opened the car door. "So this is the Point right over that hill. Come on, it'll blow your mind."

"Okay." Julia unbuckled her seat belt and stepped outside. "Who was the music you were playing?"

"Bad Religion." Brett walked over the hill and into the trees. "Yeah, they're totally my favorite band. You know, besides the Beatles."

"You didn't even know Paul McCartney was *in* the Beatles. You thought it was Paul *Simon*. You're a funny bunny."

"I'm a funny *bunny?*" Brett laughed. "Oh God, I am *not* a funny bunny."

"You're blushing. Look at you."

"All right, fine, I'm *blushing*. If you ever tell Max about this, you're excommunicated from the Cool Enough to Speak to Brett Club."

"You really think I'm cool? Wow. Nobody's ever said that to me before."

"Come on, Jules. You rock my world." Brett walked into a clearing overlooking the rocky beach below and the Pacific Ocean beyond. "So this is the Point. The army used the beach in World War Two as training grounds for invading the Nazis. Now kids just do drugs and have sex down there on the weekends, which I guess is as exciting as saving the free world."

"Wow. Wow. Wow." Julia gazed into the horizon. "It's *so* beautiful."

"What are you doing getting emancipated freshman year of high school?"

"It's just my parents. They're kind of . . ." She looked at the ground. "Well, I haven't really told Max about this, but they have a problem with drinking too much. And there was this car accident that made the *Anchorage Daily News* and they had to go into rehab for a while and all these lawyers were trying to put me in foster care, but my parents' attorney said that if I prove I can live on my own I'll get to be with them again once they're better . . . All the kids in school knew about it. I just had to get away."

"Whoa . . . I don't know what to say, Jules. Are you all right?"

"It's good they're getting help." She looked up. "Everything's going to be okay as soon as they come back home. Everything's going to be just the way it was before it got bad and I had to take care of them when they were screaming and I'd curl up in my bed and ask God to make all the scary things go away but they never did."

"When I was thirteen or fourteen, I didn't know that guys kept making semen their whole lives, so I assumed there were only fifteen or twenty ejaculations per testicle, right?" Brett smirked. "So every time I jerked off, I got on my bedroom floor and prayed that I'd make more semen because I didn't want to be sterile and never have kids, you know? I guess I realized sooner or later that I wasn't running out of ejaculations, and that's when I stopped believing in that cheap bastard God. You hear me, You dirty pig-fucker?"

"Okay . . ." Julia laughed. "Well . . . um . . . I guess I'm glad everything still works for you."

"Well . . . I . . . I guess Brett's always had his moments, but deep down he's really a good guy. I just can't believe he'd actually leave Ashley at the abortion clinic like that."

"Don't say I didn't warn you, Max." Trevor put the BMW back into gear. "Isn't it the least bit possible that he only spends time with you to feel better about himself? I've heard how he teases you in front of his *real* friends. You seem like a decent enough kid. I'd hate to see you catch his knife in the back too."

"God, it's so *boring* here." Ashley lay in the hospital bed, flipping through a copy of *The Catcher in the Rye* from the Reading Shelf. "What do you people *do* all day?"

"Pretty much the same thing," Girl-Meat picked at a hangnail. "Breakfast at nine. Group at ten. Lunch at twelve. Therapy at one. Meds at two. Afternoon activities from three to—"

"Never mind." Ashley tossed the book onto the floor and draped a pillow over her face. "I just want to go *home*."

"I used to write poetry too. Nothing amazing—'life sucks,' 'fuck the world,' wannabe-Goth shit like that—except I can't even write anymore for some reason with the electroshocks. The doctors said it would help even out my neurotransmitters, but I can't even remember how to *write* anymore. I don't know, I think I just lost that part of my *brain* or something."

"How long have you *been* in this place?"

"Four years." Girl-Meat pulled out the hangnail, then sucked on her bloody finger. "Came in on my twelfth birthday."

"Four *years?* The doctor said the program was only fifteen *months,* didn't he?"

"Well, it *gets* repeated." Girl-Meat rolled her eyes. "Group, classes, motivational speakers, again and again and again until you want to fucking kill yourself worse than you did in the first place. And all the while you're surrounded by *other* people who want to die and they actually expect you to get *better?*"

"Don't you even *want* to get better? How could you stay here for *four years?*"

"Oh, please. You preppy Pike & Crew bitches are some of the most fucked-up people in the world. What was it, Mommy's pills? Cleaning bottles under the sink? Boyfriend dump you for Tiffany the Cocksucking Cheerleader from Hell?"

"Pills," Ashley whispered. "My mom's pills."

"Fucking typical," Girl-Meat snickered. "You dippy cunt."

* * *

"Thanks a lot for hanging out with me today, Brett." Julia unlocked her apartment door. "It was all really fun except for the part where I thought I was going to die on your skateboard."

"Hey, the law of gravity isn't *my* fault. And besides, near-death experiences are only fun the first ten or twelve or fifteen times."

"Well, excuse me for not sharing your *death wish*." She laughed. "So you've had a lot of experiences like that?"

"The best was definitely this overnight biology trip freshman year. Our teacher took like ten of us out to this island two or three miles off the coast, right? And after we got there and unpacked our bags, we walked down to the beach and ran into this creepy loner type who starts hitting on my girl—my *ex*-girlfriend Quinn, tells her to come to his cabin for cigarettes and beer, shit like that. So this weirdo goes away and I tell Quinn that he's going to knife us all for sure later. You know, just a harmless joke, right? Well, that night we go back to the beach because that's when it's low tide and all the jellyfish and octopuses are on the rocks, but this half-blind girl in my class is having trouble in the dark with her walking stick, so the teacher tells me to lead her back to the cabin. When we get there I swear to God the Killer is lurking inside, so we duck into the bushes. He turns off all the lights, and this goddamn *blind* girl tells me we should step onto the *porch* because her blind women's self-defense class taught her to stay in the light if she's in danger, right? So I tell this blind retard, 'No, we're *not* going into the light. We're going to *find everyone else* and tell them about the *Killer* in our *cabin*.' Except the tide had come in and we couldn't find anyone, and they were all so far out that the water would've trapped them on every side. So here I am, cowering in fear, the biology teacher and all my friends are apparently dead—not to mention the girl I'm in love with—and I'm stuck with this blind piece of shit, plus it's getting cold enough to catch hypothermia. So I keep telling myself to go back inside the cabin and face the Killer man to man, because I'd rather die *warm*, right? But eventually we find this old two-story house on the other side of the island, so I go inside, wielding the blind girl's walking stick as a weapon, and just as I reach the top of this dark, creaky staircase, the goddamn Killer leaps out of the shadows. And he just stands there *grinning*, then finally holds out this shaking, craggy hand and says, 'You kids forgot to turn your lights off. So I did. You're welcome.'"

"*Oh my God, Brett*," Julia exhaled after a long pause. "So everything turned out okay? What about everyone else? What *happened?*"

"Nobody drowned. They were just off roasting marshmallows the whole time."

"Oh my *God*." She laughed. "That story is *amazing*, even though you really shouldn't say such mean things about people who can't see."

"Whatever you say, Jules . . . So you don't have a boyfriend back home or anything, do you?"

"No . . . not really." She blushed. "Nothing like that."

"All right . . . listen, Julia, you're really, really special. And I've said that to lots of girls and didn't really mean it, but you're not *like* any of them. God, that sounds so trite, but you know what I mean, don't you? You're just different in a really, really good way."

"Oh . . . thanks . . . you must have girls throwing themselves at you all the time."

"They're just carbon copies. Even Quinn, she's just another high school clone. You're *different* though, Julia. I *know* you're different."

"Sometimes I wish I could be one of them." She looked down at the hallway floor. "Sometimes it's so hard to be happy when you're not one of them."

"When Quinn was too drunk to stand up one time, she told me that she looks herself over in the mirror for two hours every morning before school, trying to stretch her smile out so she can look happy all day long. That's not happiness."

Silence.

"God . . ." Brett laughed. "I have this recurring dream where our school gets shot up like Columbine, and of course I turn into an unstoppable ninja warrior and take down all the shooters one by one. Quinn throws herself at me for being such a hero."

"You're just friends now? What happened?"

"She's head over heels for this fucking nimrod Trevor Thompson because he's *so* rich and *so* cute and *so* famous. She doesn't even *know* about the time he got this girl Ashley Iverson preg—"

"Wait, Trevor *Thompson* goes to your *school?* Oh my God, that kid annoys me *so much.* I mean, okay, he's made all this money and I guess he can do whatever he wants with it, but personally I don't think I could even *live* with myself if I didn't give it away to the people who really need it."

"Wow . . . You're like the nicest person I've ever met, even *with* the occasional Communist leanings. Plus you've got these really captivating green eyes."

"Oh . . . you're very charming . . ." She reddened as Brett's lips approached hers. "You're a really nice person too."

"Oh, Quinn darling, I'm home at last." Trevor opened the front door of his penthouse apartment and unbuttoned his overshirt. "It's been a long day to say the least, but I'm glad I can always come back to your sweet face and tender kisses."

He walked to the kitchen and filled a glass with cold seltzer water. "Of course, I'll be away on business tomorrow—another press junket in the Big Apple—but I have no doubt you'll still be here waiting when I come back."

He stepped into the bathroom and removed a fourteen-milligram vial of gamma hydroxybutyrate from the cabinet beneath the sink.

"Will you pretend to be kissing the lips you've been missing?" He entered the darkened bedroom and sat on the edge of the mattress. Quinn lay bound and stripped, saliva dripping from her mouth and dried semen spread across her breasts. "Will you hold your pillow and pretend I'm still there to cuddle you? Will you, Quinn?"

Beeeeeeeeeep!

"Always when things are just heating up." He picked up the cordless telephone. "Yes?"

"Hello, Trevor, this is Mrs. Kaysen. Quinn left your number with us last night before the prom and . . . well, I hope you're not busy at the moment."

"No interruption at all, Mrs. Kaysen." He emptied the translucent vial into the seltzer water. "How are you this evening?"

"Well, Quinn's father and I are very concerned. She never came home last night, and we thought she'd just gone to a party, but it's getting late and she still hasn't come home. Oh God, Trevor, I hope you don't feel that I'm accusing you of anything—Quinn's father and I both know what a wonderful kid you are—but if you have *any* idea where our daughter could possibly *be* right now . . ."

"Well, golly, Mrs. Kaysen, I know she left the party last night with a few of the older boys from school. I sure do hope the authorities find her soon." Trevor pried open Quinn's mouth and trickled the seltzer water down her throat. "Hopefully they'll get the bastards who did it without too much of a chase."

"Did what? You don't think Quinn's been *hurt*, do you? You don't think anything's *happened* to her, *do* you?"

"You never know these days, Mrs. Kaysen." He pinched Quinn's lips together and tilted her head upward, then reached for his digital camcorder. "What with the rapists and the darkies running wild at night, it's hard to know about *anything* anymore."

"Check it out, baby, I just ran away from *Solitary.*" Skin sneaked into the Youth Ward bedroom and closed the door. "Only a couple minutes till the nurse comes around for checks—I wanted to see you so bad I couldn't help it."

"Pookie-poo!" Girl-Meat chirped, skipping across the bedroom and throwing her arms around Skin's shoulders. "Pookie, this is my new roommate, Ashley. She's kind of a preppy bitch, but I like her enough to keep her alive."

"Hey, I'm Skin. How's the incarceration going?"

"It's . . . it's okay . . ." Ashley tried not to stare at his scarred face. "How'd you . . . um . . . get that name?"

"The kids at school gave it to me when I turned fourteen. The fucking zits wouldn't go away, so basically I doused my face with gasoline from my dad's lawnmower."

"*Oh my God,*" Ashley said. "You actually *did* that? I mean, I've had a few zits before and it's always really embarrassing, but I'd never . . . God . . ."

"You wouldn't know." Skin sat on the bed beside Girl-Meat and jammed his hand up her plaid miniskirt. "I've had a few zits on my face *at a time* for *five fucking years.* Do you know what it's like to be *ashamed of your face* for *five fucking years?*"

"It's all right, baby," Girl-Meat moaned. "You're still my wild sex muffin. Oh, oh there, there, right there."

"Talked to the janitor. He's going to help us out with the slushies. Tomorrow night for sure."

"Wait, I'm confused," Ashley said. "You're making *slushies?*"

"Um-hmm." Girl-Meat smiled, eyes closed. "Antifreeze slushies."

Twenty-first century digital boy, don't know how to live but I've got a lot of toys. Brett parked the Camry in the driveway as Bad Religion's *Against the Grain* played in the dashboard stereo. *My daddy's a lazy middle-class intellectual, Mommy's on Valium, so ineffectual, oh yeah, ain't life a mystery?* He removed the key from the ignition and opened the car door.

"Please be asleep, please, God, be asleep."

He unlocked the front door of the darkened house and tiptoed upstairs to the kitchen.

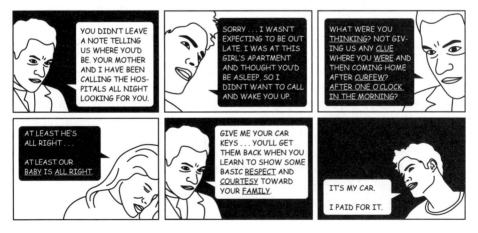

"You hand them over right now." Mr. Hunter extended his shaking hand. *"You hand them over right now, do you hear me?"*

"Fine, you overbearing asshole." Brett flung the key chain. *"Why don't you just get it over with and put a fucking noose around my neck?"*

"You never speak to me with that tone of voice again, goddamnit. Anything I tell you to do, you do with a goddamn smile on your face. Is that clear?"

"Please stop *fighting*," Mrs. Hunter cried. "Brett, please, *listen* to your *father.*"

"Do you see what you did?" Mr. Hunter screamed. *"Do you see how your mother is crying because of what you did?"*

"You're insane, Dad, even Mom thinks so. You're scared of him, aren't you, Mom? He's fucking *crazy* and you *know* it and you're *scared* of him, *aren't you?"*

"Your *brother* never talked like that," Mr. Hunter said. "Your *brother* made us *proud* to be his parents."

"You've got a real small dick, Dad, you know that?" Brett stomped to his bedroom and slammed the door. "Oh God oh God oh God no no no no no no no . . . I . . . I won't . . . I won't do it just to . . . oh God, I won't do it just to hurt him." He grabbed his childhood teddy bear and held it against his trembling chest. "Oh God, I don't want to kill myself, I don't want to kill myself, I don't want to kill myself, I don't want to kill my—"

"Last spring, University of California at Berkeley administrators
suspended a class titled Male Sexuality after investigating alle-
gations of genital photography, class orgies and field trips to
strip clubs. Class members enjoyed a visit from a dominatrix,
the viewing of porn and discussions on topics such as 'Why we
masturbate.' And the genital photography? 'We didn't force anybody to do it,' insists instructor Morgan Janssen. Rather, a
Polaroid camera was placed in a bathroom at a class get-together
with a sign on the mirror that read, 'TAKE A PICTURE OF YOUR COCK AND
PUT IT IN THE BAG.' Most of the eighteen-student class complied.
Afterward, the students tried to figure out what belonged to
whom. And the orgy? 'It was after class, and only involved, like,
five people,' Janssen says."

—ROLLING STONE, FEBRUARY 2003

"The percentage of AU students using alcohol and other drugs is
higher than the national average, according to the Core Alcohol and
Drug Survey, conducted by the Office of the Dean of Students. Eighty
percent of respondents stated that they had used alcohol at least
once in the last month, compared to the national average of 72 percent. . . . Forty-three percent drink more than five times a week."

—THE AMERICAN UNIVERSITY EAGLE, NOVEMBER 25, 2002

BEN B., 19

ALBANY, NY

"One time when I was fifteen, I was playing basketball with this kid a few years older than me who'd already been to college, and he was telling me about sleeping with this girl in her dorm room on the top bunk. But then her roommate came in and said she wanted a piece too. So he wound up fucking one girl at a time, just going back and forth from bunk to bunk until he came all over the one on the top. And I was fifteen when he told me this, so it was just like, 'Holy shit,' you know?"

"Although AU is home to many couples, some think the college years
are not the time for monogamy. 'You're trying to grow up too fast.
It just won't work,' sophomore Michelle Black said. Some also warned
against getting too serious with someone new. 'There's this line of
infatuation people cross without realizing it. That's unhealthy,'
said freshman Michael Whitney. . . . Hooking up may beat out dating
because in a relationship a student must devote a certain amount of
time from his or her daily routine to another person."
—THE AMERICAN UNIVERSITY EAGLE, OCTOBER 10, 2002

"Members of a University of Maryland, College Park, fraternity
could face criminal charges now that an autopsy has concluded that
a student pledge died from alcohol intoxication. . . .
Investigators have said charges in the case could range from hazing
to manslaughter. . . . [19-year-old Daniel] Reardon's death was the
second fatality on the university's Fraternity Row in six months."
—THE ASSOCIATED PRESS, MARCH 27, 2002

"There is a code of silence among some fraternity men on
campus. . . . In 1988, the Tampa Tribune reported on a young
woman who was allegedly gang-raped at Florida State University by
four fraternity members. They allegedly left her naked in the
hallway of a neighboring fraternity house with the fraternity's
letters written inside her thighs. Not one member of the [150-
man] fraternity would testify against his fellow brothers."
—THE UCLA DAILY BRUIN, OCTOBER 8, 1999

"In the early morning hours of February 27, Lisa Gier King and
another woman performed as exotic dancers during a Delta Chi fraternity party at the University of Florida in Gainesville. . . .
King charged that she was later raped by [a] fraternity member . . .
while two or more men watched, assisted and videotaped the
rape. . . . King claimed that [the fraternity members] would 'break
her neck' if she fought. . . . According to NOW chapter members who
have seen the tape, it appears that King is being choked [and
asked], 'What do you want? Your circulation back?' The men titled
their tape 'The Raping of a White-trash, Crackhead Bitch.'"
—THE NATIONAL NOW TIMES, FALL 1999

"Fraternity boys occupy a sacred space in American culture. Like
newlyweds, ballerinas and precocious kindergartners, we allow them
certain luxuries, forgive their mistakes with a knowing chuckle, and
tolerate their alternate universe with all its smug preening, empty
dogmatism and cocky certainty of its own importance in the larger
scheme of things. We keep their self-congratulatory rituals and
hijinks safe from the harsh realities of the real world. . . . Our
culture is so taken with youth and so committed to the preciousness
of the college experience that we rarely stop to ask what kinds of
men are created inside these self-governing Dude Biospheres."
—SALON.COM, APRIL 17, 2003

"For many young people these days, the only time they've ever gone
out on a formal date was their high school senior prom. . . . one
[student] said that his generation just happened to come along during a time of transition. A generation ago, there was one set of
courtship rituals. Twenty years from now, he continued, there will
be another. But now there are no set rules. There is ambiguity.
Ambiguity and fluidity are indeed the key traits of the current
social scene."
—THE WEEKLY STANDARD, DECEMBER 23, 2002

MARTY BECKERMAN GOES TO COLLEGE

Participates in Numerous Wholesome Activities and Even Manages to Learn Something Very Special about Himself in the Drunken, Orgiastic Process

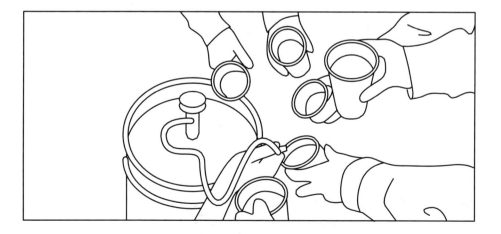

The Washington, D.C. fraternities depicted in the following piece indeed have actual names, but unfortunately these must be omitted in the present volume. This decision was made grudgingly, of course, but in all honesty the Author would rather not have to deal with potential legal issues and/or being sodomized on a cold, hard basement floor, soaking in a copious pool of frat boy vomit for thirty-six consecutive hours whilst being given no physical nourishment whatsoever, save for the negligible level of absorbable protein found in fresh Human Semen.

You see, shortly after this piece ran on the front cover of _The New York Press_ on November 14, 2001, the Author began receiving a series of letters and phone calls from American University fraternity members, all along the lines of "Marty Dies Tonight," "Get ready to lay on your stomach, faggot journalist" and "Hey Beckerman, this is Jack from Phi ████ █████ and I just want to let you know we're gonna bash your fuckin' head in with a baseball bat the next time you walk outside, so look forward to that."

Now, considering the Author still attends American University at the time of this writing, it simply wouldn't be prudent of him to further identify these fraternities in print. However, the Reader is assured that—as dictated by the First Holy Covenant of Anti-Journalism—all events and quotes depicted herein are accurately transcribed and entirely factual. Thank you for your understanding.

"It ain't a _real_ fuckin' party till you add some _Greek fuckin' letters_," Beefy declares, heaving his bloated arms around a couple of his wasted frat brothers and spilling cheap beer all over the place. "You know what I'm fuckin' _sayin'_, dogs?"

"Fuckin' _right_, dog," replies Beefy's buddy to the left, dopey smile plastered across his hideously chubby face.

"_Phi_ ████ █████ _forever!_" screeches the Other Brother, vocally confirming allegiance to his wonderful dues-paying friends and every beautiful thing their brotherly unity represents.

The two-story brick frat house, unbearably torrid with bodily heat, is filled to an uncomfortable (assuming you're not bisexual) maximum capacity. At least two hundred people lend their presences to this wretched inferno, all downing either crappy beer from the keg out back or multicolored Jell-O shooters: Plastic cups of fruity gelatin mixed with whiskey instead of water. Unconscionably loud rap music blares from speakers approximately twice the size of my dear grandmother, and the halls are replete with young men and women partaking in the drunken, ancient ritual of Freak Dancing—otherwise known to most of the general adult population as Wild Dry Humping. (Which is actually kind of interesting when you think about it, seeing as how I just wrote "my dear grandmother" and "Wild Dry Humping" in the very same sentence.)

"Are you a freshman?" a striking brunette girl asks, tapping/squeezing my shoulder and smiling with the knowledge that I—like every other boy she has most likely ever met—would very much like to insert my Hungry Teenage Penis into her Scrumptious Teenage Vagina. And yes, her strapless lavender shirt certainly *would* make a snug fit on your average oxygen particle. The curves! The *curves!*

"Yeah," I say, taking a brisk swig of atrocious beer and pretending to enjoy it like a Real Man. "I'm such a freshman it *hurts*. . . . um, whatever that's supposed to mean."

"*Ohhhhhhhhhh,*" she gushes. "Freshman year is *so* beautiful. I mean, the first time you wake up next to someone and you can't remember their name or even what they *did* to you the night before, you just . . . I don't know, you just feel so *free*, you know?"

Thank you, Lord Christ. Thank you so very, very much.

"Much campus social life [in the 1920s], at large and small schools, was controlled by fraternities and sororities. Being chosen by a good fraternity—one with the most socially adept, wealthy boys, for example—was a formidable hurdle for many freshmen; to get in was to find a ready-made group of friends and comrades. . . . Getting in was easier if one had good looks, an easy-going personality, stylish clothes and a car."

—TWENTIETH-CENTURY TEEN CULTURE BY THE DECADES: A REFERENCE GUIDE BY LUCY ROLLIN, GREENWOOD PRESS, 1999

And so it was with *boundless* optimism I left the Arctic Wasteland that is Anchorage,
Alaska, for the academic halls of American University, located in sunny and terror-
ridden Washington, D.C. It's only been two and a half months now since my tearful
good-byes with parents, friends and lovers, but I must admit I've already learned many
important things here at college: For example, my own body's extraordinary tolerance
to third-rate vodka immediately following a forty-five-minute bong session.[1] And I've
been learning a few things about *other* people too: Things like just how incredibly
fucking *stupid* most other people really are. And *man,* do I mean *fucking stupid.*

Which is kind of strange, because you'd think your general opinion of the Human
Race would go *up* after having lived on a college campus for more than two months. I
mean, you put thousands of America's Best and Brightest together with experienced,
knowledgeable professors from across the globe and you'd expect something at least
semi-respectable to come out of it, wouldn't you? *Wouldn't* you? I would. I *did,* anyway.
Turns out things don't always go the way you expect. Turns out this generation really
is Doomed after all.

And it's not like I'm some hyper-Puritan fucker who gets all Holier Than Thou whenever kids drink and fuck on the weekends.[2] If you ask me, getting screwed-up and making love are just about the two most fun things in the entire *world* next to reading
comic books and skateboarding, and my only true regret in life is not doing enough of
either. But college isn't supposed to *only* be the next four years of high school for alco-

---

1 / Ha! Ha! Just kidding, Mom!
2 / It's kind of difficult to be a hyper-Puritan fucker when you first fondled a
girl's breasts inside the darkened library of a House of God. May Christ forever bless
annual Jewish youth group temple sleepovers. Luscious.

holic jocks, their miniature penises and the random drunk sluts who love them (the miniature penises); it's not supposed to *only* be about chilled Jell-O shooters and weekend hookups between nubile fucklings who mean nothing more to each other than would big juicy slabs of meat (equipped with functional genitalia); and it's not supposed to *only* be the same teenage melodrama and popularity ladders and trying to make it with every last girl on the cheerleading squad. It's just *not*.

Except, of course, that it is: According to a major survey of American undergraduates published in *Sex on Campus: The Naked Truth About the Real Sex Lives of College Students,*[3] 76 percent have had sex with a partner who was drunk or high at the time, 46 percent have had a one-night stand, 43 percent have cheated on a steady boyfriend/girlfriend, 36 percent have had sex with someone they "didn't like," 32 percent have had sex with someone they "would never call again," 29 percent have lied about themselves to get someone in bed and 30 percent of male undergrads have gotten a girl drunk or high in order to make her more open to sexual advances. (And don't forget that we're talking about eighteen-year-old kids here.)

Incidentally, a University of California at Los Angeles study shows that while 83 percent of freshmen in 1968 attended college to broaden their horizons and "develop an integral philosophy," barely 40 percent of modern students cite personal growth or learning as reasons for applying. Which probably says something incredibly profound about our emotionally hollow generation, but . . . . well, fuck it. Here's a naughty little story about trying to get some girl to sit on my face last weekend. Enjoy!

"But . . . but what if your roommate walks in?" the Girl asks, lying on my soft bed and hopelessly attempting to delay the Glorious Inevitable. The dorm room lights are dark, and it's becoming apparent with each passing moment that Our Mutual Lust cannot— *must* not—wait any longer. This is nothing short of Destiny, dear readers: Sweet Sexual *Destiny*.

"My *roommate*?" I cackle, wrapping my arms around the Girl's warm back and pulling her closer. "Oh, don't worry about *him*. He's probably off in the woods praying to his

---

precious Jew *God* or something. It's just us, darling. Just you and me and nobody else."

"But . . . but my boyfriend back home, he's—"

"Oh honey, *he's* probably cheating on *you* right now. And really, you're in *college* now. Don't you think it's time to *forget* about home a little?"

"I . . . well, I guess so . . . I just don't know if it's too soon to be . . . well, you know . . ."

"Listen, just take a deep breath and relax, okay? All I'm going to do is massage every last square inch of your gorgeous body with my wanting Hebrew tongue for forty-five minutes or so, and then we'll make sweet, sweet love for a good seven or eight hours after that. Dear Christ, that doesn't sound so terrible, does it?"

"Well, when you put it like *that* . . ." Her wet, tender lips come within millimeters of my own. (Closer . . . closer . . . *contact*.) "So . . . um . . ." she says after a minute of delightful tongue swirling and clothes-taking-off. "You really *want* to . . . well, what you said?"

"Oh, *absolutely*." I kiss and suckle my way down to her smooth, tanned bellybutton, carefully *un*buttoning her tight blue jeans and slowly—so slowly—unzipping that annoying, useless little—

"OH—MY—*GOD!!*" my Orthodox Jewish roommate abruptly shrieks, opening the door and covering his Orthodox Jewish mouth in Pure Orthodox Jewish Shock.

"*Fuck!*" I scream. "Man, we *so* need to work out a 'sock-on-the-door' policy so this shit *doesn't happen*."

"You *know* my religious beliefs prevent me from bringing girls back to the room," explains my Orthodox Jewish roommate for the millionth fucking time. "So listen, if *you're* going to have girls in here, *I'm* going to knock on the door *three times* and then I'm going to *walk in*, because it's *my* room just as much as it is *yours*. So don't be *naked*, okay?"

"Um, Marty?" the Girl asks, cowering underneath my bedspread, half-nude and visibly humiliated. "I think I should probably be getting back to my dorm now."

Fuck it all. Fuck it all to Hell.

"[College] is a bittersweet time for most parents—especially if the child is traveling far away. It is when adults must let go. It is an ambivalent time for many teens, who are thrilled to be on their own, but who, deep down, are afraid to face the unknown without the familiar, steady hand of Mom and Dad."

—"THE HARD LESSONS YOU LEARN ON YOUR OWN" BY BILL MAXWELL, THE ST. PETERSBURG TIMES, AUGUST 22, 2001

"Parents, along with their unlimited checkbooks and credit cards, were put on this earth to pay for all our stuff, alcohol included. . . . Your parents are either scum or they hate you."

—"DO SUPERFICIALITY AND MATERIALISM BELONG AT PENN STATE?" BY FRANK LAU, THE DAILY COLLEGIAN

Another weekend, another party: This time it's not a frat house, but rather the bottom floor of a fifteen-story brick apartment building five blocks from American University's main campus. Dozens of AU students are crammed inside the $2,000/month abode, most standing in line for beer. A sandy-haired frat boy wearing khakis, a red shirt and backward-facing baseball cap pumps the Keg. His name is Jack, and tonight—for many young AU scholars, at least—he's the only man on Planet Earth who matters.

"*Jack!*" shouts a girl near the front of the line, jumping up and down and flailing her arms (and Breasts!) every which way. "Jack! Jack! *Please,* Jack! *Please!*"

"Jack!" yells a big jock. "*Yo, Jack!*"

"I *love* you, Jack!" shrieks another girl. "Jack, I *love* you!"

"Well, I love you too, honey," Jack says, gazing *straight* down the girl's black Abercrombie & Fitch halter top and overfilling her red plastic cup. Beer foam spills all over her hands and wrists. She smiles. Of *course* she smiles.

"Jack, Jack, over here, Jack!"

"Jack! Yo, *Jack!*"

"Please, Jack! *Please!"*

"Over *here,* Jack! Over *here!"*

And on and on and on,

And *on* and *on* and *on,*

And *ON* and ON and *ON,*

For longer than you'd ever fucking *believe.*

"Scott S. Krueger, '01 (freshman), died last night at Beth Israel
Deaconess Medical Center, according to wire reports early this
morning. Krueger was found unconscious in his room at Phi Gamma
Delta late Friday night, apparently suffering from alcohol poison-
ing after drinking excessively during a fraternity event. He was
in a coma for three days before his death. . . . According to
Robert M. Randolph, senior dean for Undergraduate Education and
Student Affairs, 'they (the pledges) had just been told who their
big brothers were.'"

—THE MASSACHUSETTS INSTITUTE OF TECHNOLOGY NEWS OFFICE, SEPTEMBER 30, 1997

"BE A MAN AND DO IT:
SIGMA CHI FRATERNITY"

—RECRUITMENT POSTER

Fraternity brothers—or as they occasionally call themselves for some reason,
"Greeks"—have been around a *lot* longer than you might think: The nation's oldest
frat, Phi Beta Kappa, was founded in 1776 at Williamsburg, Virginia's College of
William and Mary. Alpha Delta Phi was formed in 1836, Delta Kappa Epsilon in
1846 and Sigma Alpha Epsilon in 1856. These institutions were established in
order to give male students a sense of solidarity and kinship among one another,

as well as to provide emotional support in times of desperate need. Like, say, when they ran out of liquor or something.

"Emmanuel!" your typical colonial frat boy would say to one of his brothers. "It would seem we hath no more liquor in the stead!"

"Oh Hector," Emmanuel would laugh heartily, providing Hector with some much-needed emotional support.

Anyway, somewhere along the line fraternities became miniature Secret Societies, complete with international business connections, covert handshakes and borderline-homoerotic Rites of Passage. Fraternity brothers lived together, learned together and loved together (so to speak), and their double allure of Secrecy and Tradition brought many young men into the fold. By the early 1900s, the Greek system had spread (ha! ha!) to nearly every university in America, and fraternity membership became the highest possible status symbol a young man could hope to achieve.

Which, incredibly, *isn't* an exaggeration on my part. According to the University of Minnesota's Inter-fraternity Council, forty of the last forty-seven Supreme Court justices have been fraternity alumni, not to mention forty-three chief executive officers from America's fifty most successful corporations and nearly all U.S. presidents and vice presidents since 1825, including our current Fuckhead-in-Chief.[1]

In recent years, however, fraternities have developed a generally negative "Animal House" reputation, thanks to increasing media focus on binge drinking, hazing and sexual assault, all of which are comparatively rampant in the national frat scene. To be Greek is, in the minds of many astute people, to be the Utter Scum of Humanity.

"Fraternities are an extension of high school for people who can't move past gossiping, student government and conformity," writes columnist Jeremy Gray in *The University of California Guardian.* "At least, that was the case when I was in one. . . . Fraternities are for insecure individuals who need to feel like they belong. . . . When you put hundreds of Greeks together in puffy sweatshirts, it's quite intimidating."

Of course, many in Greek circles take offense at these pervasive (and justified) stereo-

1 / A self-admitted alcoholic until over the age of forty. Goodbye, Human Race!

types. The Kansas State University Greek Affairs Office, for example, staunchly declares: "The widely held belief that a Greek experience is costly, shallow and materialistic is incredibly ignorant and unsubstantiated." But most frat boys don't even bother denying the more obvious facts of their existence. After all, why should they?

"A certain fascination with the female form should not be considered a social ill," writes Ido Ostrowsky in the November 9, 1999, *UCLA Daily Bruin.* "This unrestrained sexuality will always be a hallmark of fraternity life, and life in general. But sadly, fraternity supporters have cowered in the face of uptight critics who try to impose their puritanical points of view. . . . Let's get real: The real lure of frats is the social scene—access to parties and sexy sorority girls."

And while it won't come as news to anyone that frat boys are a bunch of violent, horny bastards who throw parties for the sole purpose of getting little girls drunk and subsequently penetrating their Naughtiest of Naughty Parts—

"Rodeo: Largely, a term related to a fraternity practice in which the male is having intercourse with a woman doggie-style, says something intended to offend her immensely and then grabs her hair while trying to maintain penetration with his penis for eight seconds before she can "buck him off."
—AN ENTRY FROM THE GLOSSARY OF SEX ON CAMPUS: THE NAKED TRUTH ABOUT THE REAL SEX LIVES OF COLLEGE STUDENTS BY LELAND ELLIOTT AND CYNTHIA BRANTLEY (RANDOM HOUSE, 1997).

—what *doesn't* get said all too often (mostly thanks to basic human decency) is that *these girls go to frat parties because they want to get drunk and laid just as badly as the frat boys themselves.* You see, according to a field study this reporter conducted by sneaking into numerous frat parties and scientifically observing the attendees' general behavior (not to mention filling himself with various chemicals that might or might not have been dog tranquilizers), he can say with the utmost confidence that the Life

Process of a College Hookup goes invariably like so:

THE LARVAL STAGE OF DEVELOPMENT:

Frat Boy approaches Freshman Girl, sitting on couch or standing near dance floor with Scantily Clad Friends. He is handsome and nice, wears cute vest or sweater and seems very interested in her. Much giggling ensues.

THE FUNGAL STAGE OF DEVELOPMENT:

Freshman Girl, accepting Obligatory Alcoholic Beverage from Frat Boy—usually rum and Coke or Jell-O shooter—realizes just how cute Frat Boy actually is. Freshman Girl and Frat Boy proceed with flirtatious touching/dancing/squeezing/stroking as both prepare for the Hookup's immediately foreseeable Coital Stage of Development.

THE COITAL STAGE OF DEVELOPMENT:

Frat Boy, within five to ten minutes of initially approaching Freshman Girl, craftily suggests heading to Nearest Bedroom and/or Shrubbery for purpose of "talk[ing] somewhere private." Fierce copulation ensues for the next several seconds.

"The life of man: solitary, poor, nasty, brutish and short."
—THOMAS HOBBES (1588-1679)

"And while I'm thinking about it, why exactly do frat boys call themselves Greeks? Is it because ancient Athenians considered the highest form of love to be that between a young boy and a grown man? Help me out here, guys. I'm confused."
—MARTIN BECKERMAN (1983-20??)

In the end, though, it's just too easy to blame fraternity brothers alone for the Decline and Fall of Academia. Sure, the Greeks propagate and glorify conformity as the ultimate social value on campus, but that's only a *symptom* of the disease, not its actual cause. Our generation's malignancy *isn't* gratuitous mass inebriation, soulless weekend hookups and total aesthetic homogeny, but rather our having nothing else *besides* these things for which to strive. Metaphorically speaking, we've been eating our every meal at McDonald's lately and haven't taken the time to *jog off* the incalculable pounds of greasy sludge coagulating inside our very own arteries. And perhaps McDonald's is a fun and delicious treat, but those who make a lifestyle out of it are simply disgusting pigs.

And even if this analogy *doesn't* make any sense, the point is there's more to human existence than one big spin on the Orgasm-Go-Round of Contemporary Adolescence. Yes, a shadowy new realm of psychosexual gratification is open to us at all times of the day and night here on campus, but does that mean we *always* have to be pouring dubious substances into our bodies and rubbing our erogenous zones against one another's like primal orgiastic *savages*?

In a word: Probably Not. As ultraconservative former FBI director and aspiring lady J. Edgar Hoover reportedly put it, back when he was still alive, "I regret to say that we of the Federal Bureau of Investigation are powerless to act in cases of oral-genital intimacy, unless it has in some way obstructed interstate commerce."

Quite possibly, truer words have never been spoken.

↗ S.L.U.T. STATS

79%:
Percentage of 13- to 18-year-olds who have taken a sex education course

69%:
Percentage of 13- to 18-year-olds who oppose federal funding for "abstinence only" education programs

42%:
Percentage of 13- to 18-year-olds who believe public schools do not adequately teach about sex

41%:
Percentage of 13- to 18-year-olds who believe parents do not adequately teach about sex

73%:
Percentage of 13- to 18-year-olds who believe high school health centers should distribute condoms

63%:
Percentage of 13- to 18-year-olds who believe "virginity pledges" are not an effective means to prevent teens from having sex until marriage

[Source: *Time*/MTV, October 7, 2002]

JESSICA A., 19
PORTLAND, OREGON

"Usually the reason I let guys fuck me is because I'm tired of sucking their dicks."

"Thanks to a $2.3 million federal grant over three years secured
by the city's Department of Health in July, teachers in several
junior high schools this month plan to kick off a curriculum empha-
sizing saving sex until marriage. Federal provisions for the new
classes follow the 'abstinence-only' format—that is, they prohibit
discussion of birth control, except in the context of failure
rates. . . . Finally, the program will attempt to sell teenagers on
'second virginity.' . . . 'I think sex is a good thing,' says a 17-
year-old now pregnant with her second child, adding that abstinence
education sounds 'kinda dumb.'"
—THE WASHINGTON CITY PAPER, OCTOBER 25, 2002

"Wilmington, DE—Brian Peterson Jr. and his girlfriend Amy
Grossberg will appear in court together Tuesday to be arraigned on
first-degree murder charges for killing their newborn son. The
baby was found in a Newark, Delaware, motel trash bin in
November. Peterson and Grossberg, both 18 years old, have been in
jail without bail because Delaware law does not allow bond for a
defendant in a capital case. An autopsy found the boy died of a
skull fracture."
—CNN, JANUARY 20, 1997

"HOP ON HIS EROTIC EXPRESSWAY: When you want chest-heaving,
chandelier-shaking, gotta-have-it-now action, take the path of
least resistance: Cut to the carnal chase and zoom in on his hot
spots. . . . Take a cue from Christa, 25: 'If I feel really
wild, I'll push him down, rip his pants off and devour him like
an animal.'"
—COSMOPOLITAN, FEBRUARY 2002

"Should You Tell Him You're Not a Virgin?"
—SEVENTEEN COVER HEADLINE, NOVEMBER 1999

↗ S.L.U.T. STATS

86%:

Percentage of 12- to 15-year-old girls who read *Seventeen*

13%:

Who read *Cosmopolitan*

56%:

Percentage of 16- to 19-year-old girls who read *Seventeen*

31%:

Who read *Cosmopolitan*

[Source: Simmons Teen-Age Research]

$135 million:

Amount of taxpayer money George W. Bush has proposed Congress spend on federal abstinence education programs per year

[Source: *Time*, October 7, 2002]

LEORA TANENBAUM

AUTHOR OF *SLUT!: GROWING UP FEMALE WITH A BAD REPUTATION*, SEVEN
STORIES PRESS, 1999
[QUOTED FROM A JULY 21, 1999, SALON.COM INTERVIEW]

"I think girls are getting mixed, contradictory sexual messages. On the one hand, that they should be sexually active, sexually curious. At the same time they are told that they shouldn't have sexual desire, that it is slutty. . . . A large part of why girls feel like they can't say no is tied to the fact that they can't say yes. If you say yes, you're a slut. If you say no, you're a prude or a loser."

MONDAY

↗ MONDAY

"Don't want to go to schoooooool." Max blindly reached for the blaring alarm clock. "Don't want to . . . go to . . . *unnnnnnnnngh."*

He rolled off the bed and tugged the alarm clock's electrical cord from the wall socket behind the dresser, then staggered to his Dell Dimension XPS computer.

There are 5 unread Mail messages in your Inbox, declared the Microsoft Outlook Express toolbar, listing e-mails with the subjects: "Feel Like A Man Again!" "Asian Sluts, Yellow Cunts!" "Teen Bitches Swallow Your CUM Right NOW!" "GUARANTEED to Make Your Penis Bigger!" and "Rip Fluffy Sheep Apart With Your Big Shaft!"

"Sheep?" Max deleted the junk e-mails and walked to the bathroom. *"Fluffy freaking sheep?"*

He stripped out of his pajama bottoms and turned the shower knob.

Beeeeeeeep!

He sighed and stepped out of the shower, shivering from the abrupt temperature change, then wrapped a towel around his waist and walked to the front door.

"Sorry, I'm a little early." Julia stood in the hallway. "I was just getting nervous about my first day at school and . . . oh . . . um . . . um, Max?"

"What? What's wrong?"

"You're . . . you're kind of falling out, I think."

"Falling—?" He looked down at the spread-open towel, displaying a full view of his dripping wet genitalia. "Oh . . . oh my God . . ." He whipped the towel around, turning a precarious shade of red. "All right, my life is officially over now."

"Don't worry, I didn't really see anything." Julia tried to appear composed. "I mean, I *did* see something, but . . . um . . . I didn't see *that* much. I mean, I'm not saying that you have a small whatever or anything because I know guys are sensitive about that even though I've never actually seen one before thirty seconds ago, so I guess I don't have much to compare it to, except what I'm really saying is it's my fault for showing up early and never mind and I'm not even standing here and this isn't happening."

"Do you want to come inside?" Max turned back toward the bathroom. "I was just about to brush my teeth and everything. It'll only take a couple minutes."

"Okay . . ." She walked into the apartment. "So . . um . . I met your friend Brett yesterday."

"Sorry, what did you say?" Max asked through the closed door. "Couldn't hear you."

"Oh . . . oh, nothing. It's nothing."

"So what classes do you have today?"

"Let's see, one sec." She unfolded the schedule from her back pocket. "Economics, biology, P.E., precalc and Shakespeare."

"Who do you have for Shakespeare? Lovelace?"

"Right, Lovelace. Why, is she a good teacher?"

"I'm actually doing a big presentation on *Brave New World* for her class today."

"We have a *class* together? That's great, Max. I was getting worried I wouldn't know anyone in any of my classes. And I get scared when I'm alone, especially when I'm surrounded by people who I don't know or it's late at night and I think aliens are going to abduct me."

"I really don't think you should be so nervous about your first day of classes." Max emerged from the bathroom in a gray sweater and jeans. "Our school sucks."

"Honey, honey, wake up. It's time for school." Mrs. Hunter hovered over Brett's mattress, tapping him on the shoulder. "Come on, Brett, let's get up now."

"Unnnnnnnngh, Mommmm?" He rolled onto his side and buried his head between two pillows. "One second, let me just asphyxiate myself."

"Come on, let's wake up and get out of bed." Mrs. Hunter pulled the blanket and covers away. "You can't be late for class again this semes—"

"*Whoa, whoa!*" He grabbed onto the blanket and clutched it against his lower half.

"You've already slept in longer than you should've." Mrs. Hunter tugged against the blanket. "Come on, Brett, I need to get to work soon. Please don't be difficult."

"Is there a problem in here?" Mr. Hunter stood in the bedroom doorway. He walked to the bed and yanked the sheets away from Brett, revealing the rigid morning erection beneath his Pike & Crew boxer shorts. *"You get your ass out of bed right this second like a fucking man."*

"Oh Christ, Dad." Brett rolled off the mattress. "Spare me the ex-military routine, all right?"

He walked to the bathroom and locked the door, then brushed his teeth and stepped into the shower, shivering as the stream adjusted from cold to temperate.

Lap dance blow job Quinn rubbing her tight cunt against my face coming I rub my tongue over her clit jam my fingers inside her pussy finger-fucking Quinn now Ashley tied to bedposts wet spread dripping juice down I'm fucking her tight blonde pussy she's moaning writhing humping my dick making her come Cheerleader From Party I Locked In Closet licking up down putting my balls in her mouth licking sucking spank her tight ass spread across my lap put my fist in her pussy she's swallow-

ing cum Quinn is swallowing my cum Ashley is swallowing my cum Internet Girl is swallowing my cum Julia is—

"No . . . not her." He took his hand off his penis and breathed heavily, then stroked himself again to thoughts of Quinn until ejaculating onto the shower floor.

"*Attention please, your attention please. Due to heightened security precautions, unattended baggage will be inspected immediately upon seizure. In the interest of public safety, please keep your personal items by your side at all times, and do not accept any suspicious items from strangers. Thank you again for visiting Seattle-Tacoma International Airport. We wish you a safe voyage.*"

"Worst fucking run industry in America." Trevor sat in a black leather chair overlooking the DC-10 aircraft docked outside. "No excuse for bad capitalism."

"*Now boarding Flight One-twenty-four with full service to JFK. Boarding will begin for our first-class customers in rows one through five, as well as passengers with small children or special needs requiring additional assistance.*"

"Death to the Weak." Trevor stood from the leather chair and collected his carry-on bags, then retrieved the folded boarding pass from his back pocket and approached the ticket podium.

"Sir, I'll need to see some additional identification today," said the female airline worker behind the podium. "State or military ID, Social Security card, U.S. passport or—"

"Of course, of course." He withdrew his wallet and presented his driver's license. "Anything to help keep our nation secure in these troubling times."

"All right, sir, I'll need you to step over to the side for a random body search." She pointed toward an African-American security officer standing behind a table next to the jetway entrance. "Thank you for your patience."

"I'm sorry, ma'am, perhaps you've forgotten that I'm one of your *first-class* passengers." Trevor placed one hand onto the reservations podium. "As in, your *paying-four-hundred-dollars-extra* passengers."

"Sir, according to new FAA regulations in response to the tragic events of September eleventh, all flights leaving from this airport are now required to—"

"Listen, lady, I know you're just doing your job—and that's fine—but I'm going to ask you a reasonable question very slowly, okay? Do I *look* like a dirty fucking piece of hummus-eating, Allah-worshiping *terrorist shit?*"

"Sir, is there a problem over here?" The security officer approached the ticket podium, gun at his hip. "If you'll simply come with me, we'll have you on that plane in no time."

"It's only the Fourth Amendment, right?" Trevor followed the security officer to the inspection table. "And I suppose the goddamn thing isn't leaving without me."

"Can I check the insides of your bags, sir?" the security officer asked, already unzipping Trevor's carry-on luggage. "Please take off your shoes and place your feet on the table one at a time."

"Don't worry, Batman." Trevor slipped out of his imported leather footwear. "There isn't a nuclear bomb in my shoes *this* time."

"No jokes, Mr. Thompson." The security officer inspected Trevor's shoes. "All jokes will be taken seriously in light of the tragic events of Sep—"

"September eleventh, yeah, yeah, whatever." Trevor rolled his eyes. "Good God, man, a few thousand fucking *people* die and suddenly black guys can't even laugh at the idea of white guys getting blown to *smithereens* anymore? Shit, maybe the terrorists *did* win after all."

"Please unbutton your pants, Mr. Thompson." The security officer slipped on a pair of latex gloves. "Your waistline needs to be checked for hazardous materials."

"Oh, no, you fucking don't." Trevor backed away from the inspection table. "No black man is putting his hands down *my* fucking pants as long as *I'm* not in prison."

"If you want to board that plane outside, sir," said the security officer, already reaching for Trevor's groin, "your waistline *must* be examined for hazardous materials."

"Your school looks a lot different than mine back in Anchorage." Julia followed Max through the overcrowded hallways of Kapkovian Pacific. "It's kind of *colder.*"

"What do you mean?" He carried his overstuffed notebook in one hand and a paperback copy of *Brave New World* in the other. "I thought all high schools look pretty much the same everywhere."

"Oh, I used to go to this alternative high school. Actually it's a junior high and high school, so I'd already been there for a couple years."

"So it's like boarding school or something? Because Brett says everyone who's ever gone to boarding school is addicted to cocaine and wild sex."

"No, it's a public school, but you have to win a lottery to get in because only three hundred students are admitted at a time. Anyway, we had to meet with our teachers at the beginning of each semester about what we wanted to study, and as long as it filled the basic credit requirements like history or science or whatever, we'd be allowed to design our own classes. And everybody isn't screened for weapons with metal detectors like they are here, which I can't imagine makes anyone feel comfortable enough to learn anything."

"So basically you're saying that your old high school is heaven on earth? Wow, I think I'd build a whole curriculum around playing video games."

"Actually a couple kids did get credit for playing video games last semester." Julia laughed. "Their official class goal was to measure the decline of athleticism in teenagers playing *Legend of Zelda* or *Street Fighter vs. X-Men,* but I don't think they did very much work."

"And our school looks *colder* because we're not allowed to get away with studying the fine art of electronic gaming for class credit?"

"No, it's not because of *that.* Our school just has a bunch of murals and landscapes all over the walls because the creative kids can get permission to paint wherever there's still space. It's kind of a hippie school, to be honest."

"No offense, Julia," Max said, approaching a classroom door, "but welcome to hell."

"Brant? Brant?" Ms. Lovelace called from the attendance roster. "Max Brant?"

"Present, Ms. Lovelace." Max led Julia to the back of the classroom, where two desks were still unoccupied.

"Your last name is Brant?" Julia asked.

"Ciardi? Julia Ciardi?" Ms. Lovelace called.

"Here," Julia said. "I mean, present, present."

"Yeah, it's Brant," Max whispered. "Yours is Ciardi? Nice initials."

"My teachers in Anchorage don't take attendance actually. Are you supposed to say 'present' instead of 'here,' or does it matter?"

"I don't think it really matters." Max opened his three-ring binder and retrieved the notecards for his speech. "You really didn't have to do *anything* at your old school, did you? You could just skip *class?*"

"Well, if you weren't making at least a C average, you'd be sent back to a normal public school." She pretended not to notice the Max ♥s Julia scribbled on the top notecard.

"Hunter? Brett Hunter? Okay, no Brett today. Iverson? Ashley Iverson? Oh, that's right, she's out of class indefinitely. All right, Kaysen? Quinn Kaysen? No Quinn? Trevor, are you here? Trevor? No Trevor? Hmm . . . So what's up, guys? Big party last night, or is it National Skipping Class Day and nobody took the time to tell me?"

"Actually the big party was Friday night," Max said louder than he intended.

The other students who had been at Ashley's party laughed under their breaths. One student, White Mickey—an amateur pot dealer—turned around in his seat and faced Max with a condescending "dweeb."

"Thank you for the clarification, Mr. Brant," Ms. Lovelace said. "Now as you all hopefully remember, your oral reports are due today. You were to find a book that relates to Shakespeare and present it to your fellow students. We only have forty-five minutes, so who would like to go first?"

"Yo, yo, what the shizzle, Ms. Lizzle?" White Mickey stood from his desk. "I'll get up there and do my shizzity-nick-nick."

"Wonderful, Michael. However, I'd rather not have to remind you again that 'shizzity-nick-nick' is not proper usage of the English language."

"Yo, why you gotta go disrespectin' a homeboy like that, babe-y?" White Mickey withdrew a copy of *Webster's New World Spanish Dictionary* from his back pocket. "Now listen up, peeps, this here be the dictionary of the Spanish *language,* you know what I'm *sayin'?* 'Cept the thing is I can't under*stand* muthafuckin' Spanish an' shit. I don't know how to *speaks* it an' I don't know how to *reads* it, just like I can't understand a word of my main nigga *Shakespeare* over here, muthafuckas. So that's pretty much my goddamn presentation, you cum-guzzlin' bitches. I mean, shiiiiiiit."

"Thank you, Michael." Ms. Lovelace sighed. "What a lovely treatise on the cultural universality of Shakespeare's plot structure and themes. Needless to say, you'll be receiving an appropriate grade for your astonishing performance, I assure you. Now, would anyone *else* like to present his or her choice of a *Shakespeare-related* book to the classroom? *Without* offensive, patriarchal language?"

Silence.

"There isn't a *single student* in this class who prepared for this assignment? Trust me, kids, I'm not getting rich off coming in here every morning. You know, I could've gone to med school or worked as a book editor, but *no,* I wanted to be a *teacher* and *teach* students who I thought might actually *care* about—oh, I don't know—*anything.*"

"Max, Max, raise your hand," Julia whispered. *"She's having a breakdown."*

"Um, Ms. Lovelace?" Max shot his hand into the air. "Ooh, ooh, ooh—"

"Yes, Max?" She rested both hands on her forehead. "What is it?"

"I kind of prepared a presentation on *Brave New World,* but I didn't raise my hand because nobody else did it."

"Well, thank you for volunteering," Ms. Lovelace said. "The floor is yours."

Max stood from the desk and walked to the front of the room, then opened his copy of *Brave New World* and read aloud: "Orgy-porgy, Ford and fun, kiss the girls and make them one. Boys at one with girls in peace; orgy-porgy gives release."

He set the book down. The twenty-five other students laughed nervously.

"I'm not really sure how many of you have read *Brave New World,* but basically it was written in 1932 by Aldous Huxley and it's about this future where everybody is happy. All diseases have been cured, the only poor people are the savages who live in the mountains, all anyone ever has to worry about is finding a date for the weekend and getting their futuristic minigolf games in shape. The only problem is that even though everyone is happy on the outside, their lives are all unhappy on the inside. Everyone goes on this drug called Soma whenever they feel scared or sad or alone, and books by writers like Shakespeare are banned because they don't always have happy endings, like in *Romeo and Juliet* or *Hamlet.* Everybody's free to do whatever feels good, but there's no substance or passion or honesty in their lives. And just like teenagers in our world today, the future teenagers of *Brave New World* really, really like to get naked with each other at every available opportunity."

The class burst into laughter. Ms. Lovelace reddened substantially.

Max set the book down on the teacher's desk.

"The people in Huxley's future are taught from infancy that 'everyone belongs to everyone else.' They're told that love is caused by primitive biochemical interactions, nothing more. 'Chastity means passion,' the World Controller says at the end of the book. 'And passion means instability. And instability means the end of civilization. You can't have a lasting civilization without plenty of pleasant vices.' Now, I don't want to get too personal here or anything, but I do recognize many of you from Ashley Iverson's party this weekend, so I'll assume nobody will be too surprised that—according to an extremely reliable source who would know these kinds of things—at least nineteen of the twenty-six in this class aren't virgins. To be perfectly honest, I just lost my own V-card a few nights ago, and I have to say it really is like a brave new—"

"Maxwell Brant," Ms. Lovelace shrieked. "Your *assignment* is to focus on the *book,* not *'V-cards.'"*

"Right. So why *did* all nineteen of us go all the way? Is it really just because teenagers and sex go together like peanut butter and jelly, only with more spreading and delicious stickiness involved?"

What's wrong with him? Julia thought. *He's acting exactly like Brett.*

"Or is it something deeper?" Max said. "The main character of *Brave New World* even winds up *killing himself* in the end because there's no *meaning* anymore, but nobody else *cares* or even *wants* to—"

"Julia Ciardi," Ms. Lovelace interrupted. "As our newest student, I'd like to hear what you have to say about your classmate's would-be thesis. And please, no personal stories about 'V-cards' are necessary."

"Well, I guess maybe a lot of people do have sex for bad reasons," Julia said nervously. "But I don't think it's because they're not *capable* of love or anything. I guess I'd just like to believe that everybody is capable of being able to love, because I think that's what people like Shakespeare and the Beatles are all about."

"You like the *Beatles?"* White Mickey snorted. "Fuck the Beatles."

"Very interesting, Miss Ciardi." Ms. Lovelace walked back to her desk. "Now that I'm in a better mood thanks to at least *one* student in this course, the rest of your presentations are now due on Friday. Class dismissed."

The students closed their notebooks and zipped up their backpacks.

"And Mr. Brant," Ms. Lovelace said, "you will be meeting me immediately for a *very* serious student-teacher conference."

And sanity is a full time job in a world that's always changing. Brett drove through the four-story parking garage of Grace Alliance Medical Center as Bad Religion's *No Control* played in the stereo. He parked the Camry between two idle sport utility vehicles and approached a stairwell at the far end of the parking garage, then walked two flights down and crossed a sky bridge leading to the main lobby.

"Youth ward, youth ward, youth ward." Brett scanned the three-dimensional hospital map. "All right, Psychological Services, one floor up. Rock 'n' roll."

He stepped into the lobby elevator. The doors opened on the next highest floor. He walked through a long hallway to an orderly desk, behind which sat a female receptionist.

"Good afternoon, sir. Can I help you?"

"I'm here to see a friend. Is that cool?"

"Does your friend have any kind of *name?*"

"Iverson . . . Ashley Iverson."

"Hmm . . . Iverson . . . Iverson . . ." The receptionist flipped through a black notebook labeled Inpatient Directory. "Ah, yes, Iverson. Your *name,* young man?"

"Asimov. Isaac Asimov."

"One moment, Mr. Asimov." The receptionist lifted the telephone and dialed a four-digit extension on the keypad. "Miss *Iverson,*" she scowled into the receiver, "you have a *visitor* waiting in the *lobby.*" She set the telephone down. "Miss Iverson will be down momentarily. Won't you have a *seat,* young man?"

"Fair enough." Brett backed away from the desk and sat in one of the plastic lobby chairs, gazing at the multicolored wall posters proclaiming *NOTHING WAS EVER ACCOMPLISHED WITHOUT ENTHUSIASM!* and *YOU CAN DO ANYTHING YOU SET YOUR MIND TO!*

Ashley walked into the lobby wearing her striped pajamas, followed closely by a plumpish nurse.

"You didn't need to come, Brett." She walked across the lobby and threw her arms around Brett's shoulders. "Oh God, Brett, you didn't need to come."

"Don't worry, it's not you." Ashley sat on the mattress. "This morning some kid broke his glasses and tried to slash his wrists with the shards, so now all the nurses are paranoid because I guess when one of the cutters starts up again, all the rest follow. Even though I'm not a cutter, so it doesn't even matter."

"That's really great, Ash. You're not *completely* fucked up." Brett sat on the mattress beside her. "So are you feeling any better yet?"

"Well, Brett, it's not like I'm out with the fucking flu for a few days."

"Right . . . So . . . um . . ."

Silence.

"Listen, Brett, it's not your fault about what happened with the pills, all right? It wasn't about you or Trevor or the abortion or anything to do with—"

"What about Max? Was it because he asked another girl to prom the morning after you fucked him? And I do mean *you* fucked *him*."

"It's nobody's *fault,* don't you get it? My doctor says I have a serotonin imbalance, so I just need these drugs for a while and then I'll be okay again."

"Oh please, Ash. The only imbalance you have is between the size of your gorgeous tits and the rest of your fucking body."

"I'm supposed to start taking the meds after lunch. Antidepressants, antipsychotics . . . God, I'm putting down more pills than my fucking grandmother."

"I thought the problem was you put down too many pills in the first place. Or are these the kind of pills that make you think you're *not* an S-L-U-T?"

"You wouldn't understand, Brett. It doesn't *matter* how many guys you fuck when you're a girl, because that's what makes boys *like* you even though it makes *you* not like you, but you *need* boys to like you and there's *nothing* you can do about it and I don't know about you, but I'd rather be *dead* than *miserable* for the rest of *my stupid life.*"

"Things are going to be different when we get out of high school, Ash. My brother always told me that once you leave for college, you start to wonder if it was all just a really bad dream or—"

"No, Brett, it's not *going* to get any better. Some people aren't *going* to make it out of high school."

Silence.

"So . . ." Ashley forced a smile. "How's Quinn?"

"Like I have any fucking idea. I've been hanging out with this new girl though. She's totally awesome. When she smiles it's like you're sharing some kind of amazing secret or something. Good Lord, I can't even *jerk off* thinking about her without feeling guilty inside."

"Didn't you used to ask God to give you more cum after you jerked off because you thought it never came back?" Ashley placed a hand on Brett's thigh. "No offense, but I think you definitely have some issues with your penis."

"Oh . . . issues? Well . . . I guess I . . . um. . . . Oh God, Ash, I'd still fuck you in a heart-beat, you know that, right?"

"Why else would you come here?" She moved her hand over Brett's groin. "You look so fucking good right now."

"Oh, Miss Iverson?" The nurse stood in the doorway, tapping her wristwatch. "Visiting time is over. Your friend must be on his way."

"Can't we just have a few more minutes?" Ashley asked. "We were just getting started with the *visiting.*"

"Hospital policy, I'm afraid. If you'll come with me, young man, I'll escort you back to the front door."

"Oh God, Brett, I'm so sorry." She put her arms around his shoulders. "I'm just fucked-up, all right? I'm just completely fucked-up and I don't want you to feel bad and I don't want anyone to *think* about me here, okay?"

"Miss *Iverson,* this facility *disallows* physical contact between *patients* and *visitors.* May I remind you once more that you are subject to disciplinary meas—"

"Please, Ash." Brett gently pushed her away. "Never do this again."

He followed the nurse back to the lobby, then took the elevator down to the Intensive Care Unit.

"Name?"

"Hunter."

"Seeing?"

"Hunter."

"Identification?"

Brett placed his driver's license on the countertop and walked into a room halfway down the corridor. Inside, a young man lay comatose, attached to various machines regulating his oxygen intake and circulatory function.

"You bastard," Brett whispered. "You perfect fucking bastard."

"God fucking dammit, you worthless sycophant piece of *shit,*" Trevor shouted into the Nokia cell phone. "How many times do I have to tell you that I have *no* desire to host *Saturday Night Live* unless Lorne Michaels promises to kill himself during the opening credits?"

He unpacked his black leather suitcase, relaxing in his personal suite at the Manhattan Carlyle Hotel.

"Wait, he actually said *yes* to that? Just for the *ratings* I would bring his brainchild? Great, man, sign me up! We're still doing Conan and *The Daily Show,* right? And Harry

Fling tomorrow? Okay, good. And *TRL* cancelled? Well, whatever, I didn't need to degrade myself to using MTV anyway. . . . No, no, cancel the lunch with Judith Regan, I need to get back to the West Coast for that party at my apartment tomorrow night. Yeah, she's a little over the hill, but I'd still fuck her, why not? All right, man, I've got another call coming in. Stay in touch about that Pepsi ad, okay? Optimal. Take it easy."

Trevor lay on the king-size mattress, looking out at Central Park through the bedroom window. His cell phone rang again.

"You've reached Trevor's House of Whores. Our specials are white cock and black cock, but we can also give you red cock, which tends to happen when dirty faggots don't use condoms."

"Trevor, this is your father."

"Father?" Trevor sat up in the bed, heart pounding. "What prompted *you* to call?"

"Don't be facetious. I read in *Entertainment Weekly* that you'd be in New York doing interviews. As long as we're in the same city, I thought you might want to have lunch on your old man."

"Of course, Father." Trevor gritted his teeth. "Where should we meet?"

"You like French, yes? How does Pastis in thirty minutes work for you?"

"Other side of Manhattan, but I'll see what I can do. I'll have to cancel my lunch with Dirsten Kunst, you understand, but I'm fairly sure she's fucking Josh Fartnett behind my back anyway."

"Trevor, I have absolutely no idea what you're talking about. Are these your celebrity friends? Listen, I'll meet you in half an hour."

"Well, you are at least *partially* responsible for my existence. How could I not feel obligated to see you when you've been such a positive role model in my life?"

"Thirty minutes, Trevor. We'll talk then."

Trevor turned off the cell phone and walked into the hallway, then approached the elevator doors, in front of which stood another Carlyle guest.

"Holy shit, you're Paul McCartney, aren't you?" Trevor reached out his hand to the older man. "Goddamn, I've never met a Beatle before."

"Oh my God, it's Trevor Thompson! I'm like such a huge fan, Trevor! Like the biggest fan in the world! Like, oh my God! Would you ever cut a duets album with me sometime? Abbey Road Studio is probably open right this second over in London!"

"Another time, buddy. Hey, you never fucked Yoko, did you? Was that why John was so pissed off at you the last ten years?"

"Naaaah, I always enjoyed blondes more than those Asian birds. Besides, who wants to shag the fucking antichrist?"

"That's what *I* say, bro." Trevor slapped the older man on the back. "Fuck those Satan-worshipping Asian bitches, you know what I mean? So was it cool when you wrote 'Helter Skelter' and Charles Manson thought it was a personal message telling him to kill all those people in California?"

"What do you mean, *thought?*"

The elevator doors opened. The two celebrities exchanged phone numbers and parted ways once reaching the ground floor. Trevor hailed a yellow taxi on the sidewalk.

"Corner of Little West Twelfth and Ninth Avenue," he said to the driver. "No rush or anything."

The taxi drove south from the Upper East Side through Greenwich Village, then turned west toward the meatpacking district.

"Do you realize that nothing in this city is *natural?*" Trevor asked as the taxi came to a stop on the street corner. "Christ, this is the only place in the world where I still feel *alive* anymore. Anyway, here's your cash, man. Go spend it on a brand-new copy of the Koran or some clean sheets to kneel on when you face Mecca or something."

He stepped out of the taxi and walked into the restaurant, then approached his father's table.

FIFTY-FIVE MINUTES LATE IS ON TIME FOR SOME PEOPLE, I SUPPOSE. YOU LOOK GOOD, TREVOR. STILL TOO YOUNG FOR COSMETIC SURGERY, I'M ASSUMING?

ACTUALLY I WAS GOING TO ASK YOUR BLESSING TO HAVE THE DOCTORS MAKE ME INTO A SEVEN-FOOT-TALL LATINO WOMAN.

YOU HAVE YOUR MOTHER'S LOOKS ANYWAY.... YOU'LL BE HAPPY TO HEAR THE PSYCHIATRISTS SAY SHE'S DOING MUCH BETTER.

WELL, ISN'T THAT SPECIAL? NOT THAT I CARE, BUT HAVE YOU BEEN SEEING ANYONE NEW LATELY?

ACTUALLY I HAVE A DATE AT THE ASTORIA WITH DEMI WHORE TONIGHT. OF COURSE, I'LL HAVE TO WATCH MY BACK FOR BRUISE KILLIS AND ASSTON BUTCHER. HA! HA!

CHRIST, FATHER, WHO HASN'T FUCKED DEMI WHORE? GIVES BETTER HEAD THAN COURTNEY GLOVE THOUGH. OF COURSE, IT'S INTERESTING THAT SHE ALWAYS LIKES IT STRAIGHT IN THE—

"Are you working on any new books? It's almost been a year since your last one 'hit the streets,' as you kids say."

"Don't worry, Father, the follow-up is on its way." Trevor motioned to the waiter for a glass of water. "Anyway, my last royalty check came in around four hundred and fifty thousand dollars, so I'm not too distressed about completing the new manuscript any-time in the near future."

"You know, Trevor, you shouldn't count on your writing as a lifelong career. The money might be good right now, but there's no long-term salary, no medical insurance, no retirement plan. Now, a *real* future involves a college degree, and preferably a master's at that. I don't want you coming back to me after you're nineteen and asking for a place to stay."

"Perhaps you misheard, Father. I'm earning *ten times* what the average American makes *annually* and I'm still in *high school*."

"Well, I'm happy you've found a nice hobby, Trevor, but I'm talking about your *future* here. Maybe you should start looking for a summer job?"

"Why can't you be fucking proud of me?" Trevor stood from the chair and banged on the table. "You divorce Mother and blow my college savings on your fucking *lawyers* and I make it all back *myself* to prove that I never *needed* you and you *still* can't even act like I've accomplished *one goddamn thing* except finding some *nice little hobby?"*

Silence throughout the restaurant.

"I tell people Mother is dead," Trevor said quietly. "It's easier than saying she couldn't handle having her dick husband walk out on her with all the money."

"Sir, is there a problem here?" the waiter asked.

"No." Trevor left the restaurant and walked back into the Manhattan afternoon. "Hmm, I wonder if I could actually pay to have my own father killed?" He hailed another taxi and disappeared into the ceaseless cosmopolitan matrix.

"So what did you think about your first day of school?" Max walked beside Julia on their way home.

"Oh, I thought it was okay. In the biology lab these girls wearing black capes and dog collars tried to resurrect the frog they were supposed to be dissecting . . . What did Ms. Lovelace have to say during your conference?"

"Basically that I made some good points, but stepped over the line with the whole V-card thing. I guess I was just trying to do something funny like Brett would've done, except I think he's way better at getting away with stuff like that."

Silence.

"We actually used to walk home from kindergarten this way," Max said. "And I had this Ghostbusters backpack, which I thought could trap ghosts like the Ghostbusters did in the movie and cartoons. So I'd go around the neighborhood pretending to blast ghosts all the time, and one day Brett said that if I really wanted to blast ghosts, I should call nine-one-one and say there's something strange in the neighborhood."

"He really told you to *do* that?" Julia laughed. "What *happened?*"

"Mom caught me dialing the phone and asked what I was doing, so I told her I was calling the Ghostbusters. She probably got kind of concerned."

"You're kind of like Brett in a lot of ways, you know that? Even though sometimes it seems like you're trying to be like him when maybe you should just try being your . . . um . . . I mean, *I* don't know *Brett.* What am I *talking* about?"

"Of course you know him. You two were making out in the hallway last night, so I just figured you'd probably met each other and everything."

"You . . . you *saw* us? Oh Max, no, no, you *didn't* . . . I mean, it's not *like* . . . oh God, Max, let's just talk about something else now, okay?"

"Why should we talk about something else? Prom was really special for me and I thought you had a lot of fun too."

"No, no, no, Max, I *did* have fun. Oh God, I had *so much* fun, but . . . I just need space to think about things right now, all right? I just need *space* to . . . oh God, Max, I just didn't know how to *tell* you."

"You're home thirty minutes later than I ordered, Brett." Mr. Hunter sat in front of the television, watching Fox News Channel. "We made an agreement about your car this morning. You'll be giving me your keys right—"

"—*now these are precision guided missiles—*"

"—*military installations being targeted—*"

"—*surgical strikes, not carpet bombing—*"

"Goddamn." Mr. Hunter laughed. "We're blowing the living shit out of those Arabs. . . . What did you learn in school today?"

"Not too much," Brett said, "I'm making A's and B's in all my classes in case you were wonder—"

"You spent *six hours* at an *institution of public education* and didn't learn a single thing?"

"Nope. Guess not."

"You know, back when *I* was in school, education actually *meant* something to us. It was a way up the social ladder. We didn't just fuck around with our time back then, and they were *still* the happiest days of our lives."

"Right, Dad. And now you're a bitter old man who can't even get it up anymore."

"From now until the end of the school year, I want you to come home every day having learned at least three things. For every day you do, you'll get to keep your car. Maybe then you'll actually *know* something by the time you graduate."

"Well, Dad, I just learned that you're even more of an insane asshole than I thought. Does that count?"

Beeeeeeeep!

"Yes?" Mr. Hunter lifted the telephone. "One moment. He's right here."

"Hello?" Brett took the telephone. "Hey, Jules, what's up? Yeah, I'm doing okay. . . . You mean right now? How about in a couple hours? Yeah, I don't really have a car right now because my dad suffers from post-traumatic stress disorder thanks to the Vietnam War. Okay, okay, see you later."

"The Kaysens called this morning, by the way," Mr. Hunter said as Brett set the phone down. "Apparently Quinn ran away from home without leaving any kind of note. You haven't seen her anywhere, have you?"

"Ran away from home? What the fuck are you *talking* about?"

"—and of *course* I'll do the cover again, Jann. Don't be sinister." Trevor smiled into the cell phone, waiting for the Sidewalk Café bartender to return with his bottle of Guinness. "What, you think I'm going to ditch *Rolling Stone* like you ditched your fucking wife? You're getting paranoid in your old age . . . So I should get down to Annie's studio between three and four for the shoot? Optimal, I'll catch you later. And say hi to the boyfriend for me, all right? What is he, a third of your age or something? Well, close enough, right? Ha! Ha! Keep it real, Jann."

He turned off the cell phone and swigged the Guinness.

"So are you actually Trevor Thompson?" The post-adolescent Asian girl sat on the barstool beside Trevor, wearing an NYU sweatshirt and drinking vanilla Stolichnaya thinned with milk and ice.

"Am I so obvious?" Trevor smirked.

"What are you doing in New York?"

"Interviews, photo shoots, nothing too out of the ordinary. Actually I prefer the East Coast by far."

"What do you mean?"

"Well, on the West Coast, social success is based wholly upon whether or not you're relaxed. This is because everyone on the West Coast is an ambitionless vegetable addicted to marijuana. However, on the East Coast, being stressed-out of your fucking mind is the single most important indicator of social success, since you're obviously a person with important responsibilities. Plus, New York City bartenders don't give a shit whether you're too young to legally drink . . . by the way, who the hell are you?"

"Oh, I go to NYU. I'm working on getting into modeling, but it's so hard to get your foot in the door. God, you must be living out your *dream*, Trevor. I mean, everyone in the country knows who you are, the girls all have posters of you in their bedrooms . . . And you're going out with Dirsten *Kunst* of all people. You must be like the happiest teenager in the world."

"The fame isn't important. All I really want is to accumulate as much wealth as humanly possible . . . Maybe that came from when my parents got divorced and each tried to buy my love from the other one. Of course, Mother has since become tragically dead."

"Oh my God, I'm so sorry to hear that. You must've been devastated."

"Hey, you're Asian. Is it true that Japanese businessmen pay thousands of dollars to eat sushi off the stomachs of naked teenage girls? This kid Ryu I met in Tokyo told me about a place like that, but I couldn't find it."

"I'm Korean, not Japanese."

"Well, whatever. I mean, I *like* sushi and everything, but it pretty much makes your breath reek like Hiroshima after the fucking Bomb. . . . Hey, as long as we're talking about eating off cute Asian girls, is there any chance you'd want to go check out my luxury suite uptown at the Carlyle?"

"Oh, cool! I've never been inside a *luxury* suite before!"

"Optimal." Trevor slapped a twenty-dollar bill onto the countertop for both their drinks. "By the way, you don't worship like Satan or Yoko Ono or anything, do you?"

"Check it out, babe, I just ran away from solitary *again*." Skin sneaked into the Youth Ward bedroom with a tattered backpack flung over his shoulder.

"Oh Pookie-pook!" Girl-Meat chirped, skipping across the room and kissing Skin on his disfigured cheek. "You brought the special syrup for our slushy party tonight?"

"Right here." He unzipped the backpack and withdrew a yellow canister of NAPA-brand ethylene glycol. "Good for a hundred thousand miles or three teenage suicides. Whichever comes first."

"Are you supposed to mix it with orange juice or anything?" Ashley asked. "I mean, like how you mix vodka to make it taste better?"

"Naaah, it's supposed to taste really sweet all by itself. Thirty-thousand cats kill themselves every year lapping it up because it tastes so good."

"This girl I knew in junior high tried killing herself off it," Girl-Meat said. "She had this stupid crush on one of the football players, but never even talked to him once. Then she got into all this Wicca bullshit and cast some retarded love spell on him from this old book in the library, and the next day after school he fucking raped her on the gymnasium floor. True story."

Silence.

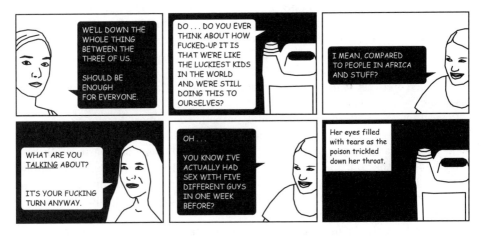

"So Julia said you want to talk?" Brett walked through the stairwell doorway onto the apartment complex rooftop.

"Fuck you, Brett." Max leaned against the steel guardrail, gazing into the darkening horizon. "You could've had any girl you wanted."

"She only wants to be your friend, Max."

"I would've *never* touched Quinn, you know that? Even if I had the chance and she was drunk like she is every weekend. Nobody deserves to have their best friend make them feel like this—"

"What do you want me to do, Max? Stop talking to her just because you've got a lit-tle fucking crush? Grow the fuck up and try being a man for once in your life, all right? Don't try to use our fucking friendship to keep me and her apart."

"Our *friendship?* You take the girl I like the same day you meet her and then tell me I'm the one using our friendship? You *knew* I liked her, Brett. I *told* you I liked her."

"So what? So fucking what? You deserve her because you met her first?"

"I don't fucking deserve her, Brett, don't you get it? After Ashley I don't deserve anyone as perfect as—"

"Would you quit *bitching* about *Ashley?* She fucked you. You fucked her. That's it, all right? It's *over* now."

"She tried to kill herself the next night. How is that not my fault?"

"Because she fucking said so, all right? It's not *your* fault. It's not *my* fault. If it's anyone's fault, it's hers for sucking off everything with a pulse and then actually feeling *bad* about it. *'Oh God, Brett, it felt so good.'* That sound familiar?"

"I fucking hate you, Brett. I swear to God I fucking hate you."

"Oh yeah?" He grabbed onto Max's shirt collar and shoved him against the steel guardrail. "Come *on,* man. It's just a fucking *girl.*"

"I love her, Brett. I love her more than you know how. You're my friend. You can't do this to me."

"Correction, Maxwell. You are so fucking pathetic sometimes."

"Please don't fight each other." Julia stood in the stairwell doorway, clutching her arms against her quivering chest. "Not over me. Please not over me." She walked across the rooftop. "I'm so sorry, Max. It's all my fault. I knew all along, all right? I knew all along you liked me and that didn't stop me and please don't blame Brett because he didn't know like I did even though you told him and didn't tell me."

She buried her cheeks in Max's chest; her tears leaked through his torn shirt.

"When I was little—I think about eight or nine—I stole some money from my mom's purse when she was passed out drunk. And it was only a few dollars, but the next day she found it in my diary and told me I could've had it if I'd just asked. And I promised myself from that point on to be as selfless as possible, but I knew how you felt and that didn't stop me."

She closed her eyes and smeared her tears across Max's cheeks.

"I didn't mean to hurt you, Max. I *never* meant to hurt you, but you need to understand that I'm no more special than any other girl you'll ever meet. And I really love being your friend—and prom was so wonderful—but it's just. . . . Oh God, Max, I think you need to get over me. That would be the best thing. Then you and Brett can be friends again and we'll be friends and everything will be okay, just like it was before."

"I . . . I don't know if . . . Julia, I don't think I can do it."

"Why *not,* Max? Why can't you just get *over* me?"

"Because you . . . you become someone more beautiful every time you laugh."

"Oh God, Max," she whispered. "I wish I could fall in love with you just like that too. I honestly wish that we could be happy together as more than friends, but I can wish and wish and I can't change the way I *feel,* and I'm so, so, so *sorry.*"

And Max knew one thing:

This was love.

And he owed it to himself to let it die.

"The last two years of high school are supposed to be about making memories. Proms, pep rallies, homecoming games and graduation parties. But for the class of 2003, two monumental events
overshadow those crucial years. The terrorist attacks of
September 11, 2001 and the war in Iraq will forever color their
high school memories. Seniors say the threat of terrorism and
the reality of America at war has changed them—they're no
longer naive; they've lost the blind fearlessness of youth; they
are forever watchful. 'We saw that we are really vulnerable,'
said Sarah Biggs, a senior at Pine Forest High School. 'It
changed us forever. We're more . . .' Sarah paused, searching
for the word. 'Cautious.'"
—THE PENSACOLA NEWS JOURNAL, MARCH 29, 2003

"Until two weeks ago, young Americans had never had it so
good. Now, with the U.S. gearing up for an uncertain war,
a question mark hangs over their future. Can they take the
pressure? . . . Not since Vietnam had Americans witnessed
bloodshed among their own people on such a scale. Since then,
bar one or two limited wars fought in foreign countries, young
people had grown up to know only peace and prosperity. The
Vietnam conflict shaped one era—will the war on terror shape ours?"
—BBC NEWS ONLINE, SEPTEMBER 25, 2001

"This catchy adage was the general consensus among area university
and high school students following President Bush's declaration of
war Wednesday evening. Generation [Y]ers say 'Just do it.' 'Right
on, take care of it,' said 19-year-old Joe Barker, a student at
Ohio University-Chillicothe. 'Do what you have to do. Like Bush
said, the risks of not doing something greatly outnumber the
risks of doing something. We need to democratize the rogue
nations.' According to Barker, most of his classmates seem pretty
'gung-ho' about going to war."
—THE CHILLICOTHE GAZETTE, MARCH 21, 2003

↗ S.L.U.T. STAT

60%:

Percentage of American teenagers who supported the 2003 Iraq War
[Source: *The Wall Street Journal*, March 28, 2003]

"A little-noticed provision in a new federal education law is
requiring high schools to hand over to military recruiters some
key information about its juniors and seniors: name, address and
phone number. The Pentagon says the information will help it
recruit young people to defend their country."
—THE ASSOCIATED PRESS, DECEMBER 3, 2002

↗ S.L.U.T. STATS

25%:

Percentage of college freshmen nationwide today who believe keeping up to date with political affairs is "very important or essential"

50%:

Percentage of college freshmen nationwide in 1972 who believed keeping up to date with political affairs was "very important or essential"
[Source: The University of California at Los Angeles]

"The community draft boards that became notorious for sending reluctant young men off to Vietnam have languished since the early 1970s, their membership ebbing and their purpose all but lost when the draft was ended. But a few weeks ago, on an obscure federal Web site devoted to the war on terrorism, the Bush administration quietly began a public campaign to bring the draft boards back to life. 'Serve Your Community and the Nation,' the announcement urges."
—SALON.COM, NOVEMBER 3, 2003

"The war has ruined us for everything. We are not youth any longer. . . . We were eighteen and had begun to love life and the world; and we had to shoot it to pieces. The first bomb, the first explosion, burst in our hearts."
—ALL QUIET ON THE WESTERN FRONT, ERICH MARIA REMARQUE, 1928

"It would have been comfortable, but I could not believe it. Because it seemed clear that wars were not made by generations and their special stupidities, but that wars were made instead by something ignorant in the human heart."
—A SEPARATE PEACE BY JOHN KNOWLES, 1959

"It is a new kind of war, and this government will adjust."
—GEORGE WALKER BUSH, SEPTEMBER 13, 2001

DISPATCHES FROM THE APOCALYPSE: SEPTEMBER 11, 2001

↗ Washington, D.C.—She looked like a corpse, her eyes rolled upward in their sockets, her tongue hanging out of her mouth. If not for her violent convulsions on the floor, we would've believed she had just died in front of us.

"Oh my God," someone in the hallway said.

We gawked at the eighteen-year-old girl's collapsed body for half a minute before racing six flights down the stairwell and screaming at the American University dormitory attendant to call an ambulance. We took the elevator back to our floor. Others had assisted the girl onto a padded chair in the student lounge.

"What's going on, guys?" she asked.

"Are you okay?" asked one student.

"I'm . . . I'm fine. Is something wrong?"

"You were just on the ground. Shaking."

"I . . . Wow, I feel fine. I really do."

"Are you epileptic?"

"No . . ."

"Diabetic?"

"No, I . . . I'm fine now. Really."

"Have you ever had a seizure before?"

"No, I'm . . . I'm just from New York."

The death toll was unofficially estimated at twenty thousand as of Tuesday evening, but is presently lowered to a quarter of that figure. It's been fifty-five hours now since the attacks in New York and Washington, and the images of airplanes crashing into skyscrapers somehow seem less shocking. For three days we've watched the television news networks air footage of jets exploding, towers collapsing, thousands falling to their deaths, the U.S. military's headquarters in flames and the creation of a debris-laden Wasteland called Manhattan.

Like many others, I was awakened Tuesday morning to screams of "Oh my God, oh my God, oh my *God.*" Half an hour earlier, at 8:45 a.m. Eastern Standard Time, armed zealots hijacked American Airlines Flight 11 and crashed it into the north tower of the World Trade Center. Eighteen minutes later United Airlines Flight 175 hurtled into the WTC south tower. Hellfire and death caught on videotape. Astronauts in space could see the plume of ash over New York City.

At 9:40 a.m. the Federal Aviation Administration halted all flight operations within the continental United States. It was the first time such an action had been taken, but came too late: Three minutes later, American Airlines Flight 77 crashed into the Army Wing of the Pentagon here in Washington, obliterating a fifth of what many believed to be the most unassailable complex in the world. Two hundred people died. Thick, black smoke filled the skies.

Twenty minutes later, back in New York, the Twin Towers collapsed to the ground, their frameworks incorrigibly melted by burning jet fuel. Thousands of human beings were instantaneously crushed under incalculable tons of steel and glass. In the streets below, screaming New Yorkers either ran north for safety or ducked under parked automobiles to shield themselves from plummeting rubble.

Ten minutes after the Towers' collapse, at 10:10 a.m., United Airlines Flight 93 crashed southeast of Pittsburgh, Pennsylvania, killing all forty-four onboard. Military officials say the flight was intended for the White House. Why it went down prematurely is anyone's morbid guess.

So the terrorists were 75 percent successful, if you want to look at it strictly as a hit-or-miss operation. Thousands were slaughtered. Any preconceptions of our nation as an impenetrable fortress went down along with the two largest buildings on our continent.

In Washington, fear has become dark and palpable. It's hidden under nervous patriotism and calls for Revenge, Revenge, Revenge, but detached paranoia and broiling hate lay dormant in everyone's tired eyes and forced smiles.

"We need to kill all the fucking Palestinians, that's what we need to do," declared one girl on my dorm floor. "I don't care if some of them are innocent. We just need to kill all the fucking Palestinians."

Which might sound like a half-sane idea if the Palestinians had actually *orchestrated* Tuesday's attacks, but—as many journalists and military officials have already pointed out—our enemy here isn't a nation but a subculture: We can bomb Afghanistan and Iraq and the Palestinian territories all we want, but it won't stop the Suicide Soldiers. They're already here.

"I still think that a piece of garbage is responsible for this," writes a friend of mine serving in the U.S. Navy. "We should wipe him and his entire country off the map so these bastards don't reproduce anymore. I understand that may sound like a Nazi solution and come back to World War Two and wiping out an entire race, but when you have women and children [in the Middle East] burning American flags and eating candy to celebrate the deaths of thousands . . . These people need to burn."

I'm writing all this from a friend's apartment terrace overlooking the Capitol, between the White House and the National Archives. American University has been evacuated for two hours thanks to multiple bomb threats, and this seemed like an appropriate place to spend the sweltering afternoon: Two days ago American Airlines Flight 77 circled over this very building before colliding into the Pentagon.

Thousands of people are dead now. The Columbine Slaughter—at one time the defining event of Generation Y—is *nothing* compared to this. *Thousands of people are dead.* People who had awkward first kisses and best friends and moms and dads and dogs and cats, and they were all *people.* And now they're Gone. Nowhere. Dead.

Black helicopters have circled over the Capitol Dome for thirty minutes now. Ambulances screech through the downtown Washington streets. A fire truck pulls in front of the National Archives, sirens blaring and lights flashing: Another bomb threat? Military police, canine patrols . . . Is this *America?*

No, this is something new. There's no going back: We're not living in the same world anymore. The Holy Land's psychotic devaluation of human life has spread to American shores. We've all been branded with a new, violent national existence.

And I find myself asking: *Is this the world my generation will inherit?*

NICK V., 18

SEATTLE, WASHINGTON

"I don't wear Abercrombie just because everyone else does. Girls just like it, you know? It's like an equalizer: You wear it and you meet this basic standard everyone agrees on, and that's how you get girls."

"Abercrombie & Fitch, the retailer that has been criticized for sexually and racially provocative catalogs and designs, is under fire—again. Several consumer advocacy groups said they have sent e-mails to A & F to protest the chain's latest offering of thong underwear in children's sizes, with the words 'eye candy' and 'wink wink,' printed on the front. . . . Last year, the youth-oriented clothing retailer angered many consumer advocacy groups with its summer and Christmas catalogs showing sexually provocative teenage-looking models apparently in the nude."
—CNN, MAY 28, 2002

"The underwear for young girls was created with the intention to be lighthearted and cute. Any misinterpretation of that is purely in the eye of the beholder."
—ABERCROMBIE & FITCH PRESS STATEMENT, MAY 24, 2002

↗ S.L.U.T. STATS

Percentage of 9- and 10-year-old girls who are trying to lose weight: **40**
[Source: *Pediatrics*, September 2003]

Revenue generated by sales of thongs to 7- to 12-year-old girls in 2000:
$400,000
Revenue generated by sales of thongs to 7- to 12-year-old girls in 2002:
$1.6 million
Revenue generated by sales of thongs to 13- to 17-year-old girls in 2002:
$152 million
[Source: *Time* Magazine, September 29, 2003]

"American girls are starting puberty earlier than most experts had thought, says a new study published today in the journal *Pediatrics*. University of Virginia pediatricians report some girls begin early signs of puberty—breast development and the growth of pubic hair—as early as 6 or 7. . . . An 8-year-old girl who looks 12 or 13 'still behaves like an 8- or 9-year-old girl, and you need to keep that in perspective,' Dr. Frank Biro said. . . . No one knows why puberty may be starting early, although doctors cite a variety of factors. Among them: increased obesity; excess protein in modern diets; and the estrogen-like effects of synthetic plastics, insecticides and hair products."
—THE CINCINNATI ENQUIRER, OCTOBER 5, 1999

"Eating disorder experts say that prepubescent girls are developing eating disorders as young as five and six years old, and they may be acquiring their obsession from parents who are preoccupied with their own body images, and media images of skinny pop stars. Experts say the problem among children is growing. . . . Justine Gallagher was 5 years old when she started eating paper in order to lose weight. She ate up to 10 pieces of paper a day, believing that filling up on paper—rather than food—would help her lose weight. The boys at school were telling Justine that she was fat. Meanwhile, her teachers noticed that parts of her books were missing."
—ABC NEWS, DECEMBER 19, 2001

↗ S.L.U.T. STATS

Number of teens under 18 who received cosmetic surgery in 2001: **79,501**
Number of teens under 18 who received fake breasts: **3,682**
Number of teens under 18 who received reshaped noses: **29,700**
Number of teens under 18 who received reshaped ears: **23,000**
Number of teens under 18 who received liposuction: **2,755**
Number of teens under 18 who received fake breasts in 1994: **392**
Number of teens under 18 who received liposuction in 1994: **511**
[Source: *Branded: The Buying and Selling of Teenagers* by Alissa Quart, Perseus Publishing, 2003]

↗ S.L.U.T. STATS

Percentage of high school students with anorexia/bulimia: 11
[Source: Children Now]

19.7%:

Percentage of the nation's alcohol consumed by underage drinkers
[21 and under]

$22,500,000,000:

Total sales generated by underage alcohol consumption in 1999
[Source: The Columbia University National Center on Addiction and Substance Abuse,
February 2003]

"The home-alone drinking party is nothing new on the suburban teen scene, and there's always a kid or two showing up drunk at the high school dance. But this year in Westchester County, a prosperous suburban area north of New York City, one youngster died at an unchaperoned bash, and as many as two hundred high schoolers showed up drunk at a homecoming dance. These and other startling episodes of underage drinking have officials searching for answers and parents worried more than ever—including concerns about a possible link between youngsters' drinking and the adults' affluent lifestyle."

—THE ASSOCIATED PRESS, NOVEMBER 16, 2002

TUESDAY

"Welcome back to the big show, everyone." Seventy-year-old television legend Harry Fling looked into the studio cameras beaming his likeness into sixty-five million homes worldwide, adjusting his trademark suspenders and horn-rimmed glasses. "For those of you just joining us today on *Harry Fling Live,* our special guest is the seventeen-year-old financial guru whose book *Investing for Teenagers* has topped the *New York Times* bestseller list for fifteen weeks. A new one, *I Made a Million Dollars Before Turning Eighteen and So Can You: How to Conquer the Stock Market AND High School,* is in the works. The magazine *Teen People* recently voted him one of the twenty teenagers most likely to change the world, and the adult version of that publication has declared him the Sexiest Man Alive for the second consecutive year. He's a favorite pinup of preteen girls nationwide and a business-savvy midadolescent media magnate. Ladies and gentlemen, *Trevor Thompson.*"

"Thanks for all the kind words, Harry." Trevor smiled into the cameras. "Glad to be in New York."

"You're the toast of Manhattan, Trevor. Author Kurt Vonnegut recently said that *Investing for Teenagers* will do for your generation what *Slaughterhouse-Five* did for his. How does it feel to be in the eye of the pop-culture storm?"

"Well, I've been so busy lately I haven't been able to just kick back and savor the fruits of my success. But it feels good, man. Probably as good as it felt when you divorced your seventh wife."

"You've got that straight, homeboy. Now, Trevor, millions young and old alike read your work. The *Wall Street Journal* last month ran a cover story calling you the first great mind of your generation. Georgetown University is offering an entire course based around the socioeconomic theories presented in *Investing for Teenagers*. How does it *feel?*"

"Well, Harry, I don't know whether or not I'm the first great mind of my *genera-tion*," Trevor laughed. "I mean, okay, *maybe* I am, but the response to the book has definitely been humbling, you know? And in all honesty I'm a pretty normal guy at the end of the day. I've got a new girlfriend waiting for me back home, my own apart-ment, a supercool BMW prototype. . . . Nothing too spectacular, Harry. And really, this is a generation suffering from a *lack* of great minds, so if I'm a hero to the masses then all the better for everyone."

"So despite the ceaseless media attention and countless accolades, Trevor Thompson refuses to place himself on a pedestal above his clearly worthless peers. Ladies and gentlemen, that's either ignorance or class, and as someone who knew Frank Sinatra intimately, let me tell you that is *class*. You are a god amongst beasts, young man."

"Thanks, Harry. You know, the transcontinental celebrity isn't of much importance to me. Honestly, fame is no different than popularity in high school. You can get away with any damn thing you please, simply because other people are envious and fasci-nated by the insularity of your lifestyle. Life is circular, Harry. Patterns repeat."

"Trevor, this nation is absolutely *dying* to know: What's your secret to financial conquest in these times of economic recession?"

"Well, Harry, basically success in the free market isn't about how your companies are actually *doing*. It's just how people *think* they're doing. Like the whole nineties dot-com boom: None of those companies were making any money at all, but everyone *thought* they were the future of global commerce. All I did was buy into as many start-ups as possible and then sell before the inevitable crash. The execs at Enron did basically the same thing, except they used privileged information as opposed to their own natural intuition. Ethics are needed for capitalism, and ethical capitalism is what's needed for humanity. Not Marxist socialism, as some of my fellow students believe, having never read a history book. The free market is the only system that works, but it must be guided by ethical men."

"Such wisdom, such *youth*. Tell me, Trevor: What about the anal sex?"

"Sorry, what was that, Harry? I'm still a little jetlagged and thought you just asked something you couldn't have possibly asked."

"New studies show that at least *twelve percent* of American fourteen-year-olds are bumping it in the booty, Trevor. This was in *U.S. News and World Report,* for Christ's sake. What does it *mean?* What does it *mean,* Trevor?"

"God, Harry, I don't know. Actually I kind of have this wholesome public image to keep up for Middle America, so why don't we just talk about something besides sodomy until the next commercial or whatev—"

"Have you heard of the organization True Love Waits? It's a Christian nonprofit based out of Nashville, Tennessee, which encourages teenagers worldwide to sign its 'virginity pledge.' However, all these young boys and girls are defining sexual intercourse only as penile/vaginal penetration, so the rates of teen and preteen anal sex are skyrocketing through the freaking stratosphere. What's your opinion on this scandalous development, Trevor?"

"Christ, Harry, I don't think anyone should be forced to do anything they don't want. . . . Why are we talking about this again?"

"Well, Trevor, I've been thinking about leaving my eighth wife soon. Is it likely that some nineteen-year-old nymphet would possibly welcome Big Harry's scepter into her blooming teenage rectum?"

"Good *Lord,* Harry. Can't we talk about my new *book* or something?"

"Glorious teenage rectums, yes, yes, so precious, so, so precious . . ." The television host twiddled his fingers, a bead of saliva dripping down his haggard chin. "All right, Trevor, we need to go to commercial break, so hold on to that last thought for now. This is *Harry Fling Live,* everyone. Our guest is teen author and staunch anal sex *proponent,* thank God, Trevor Thompson. We'll be back in a moment."

"What the fuck are you saying, you sick bastard?" Trevor screamed as the cameras faded to black. *"Staunch?"*

Things are getting tougher when you can't get the top off the bottom of the barrel; wide open road of my future now, it's looking fucking narrow. Brett smoked a Camel Turkish Jade with trembling fingers as Operation Ivy's *Energy* played on the idle Camry's sound system. *All I know is that I don't know, all I know is that I don't know nothing, all I know is that I don't know, all I know is that I don't know nothing.*

The morning bell rang inside the school building. All the students in the parking lot dashed inside.

"Fuck it." Brett took a drag off the Camel, exhaling smoke out the open window. "I'm finishing this goddamn cigarette."

He flicked the filter onto the pavement and opened the driver-side door. *All I know is that I don't know nothing, and that's fine.* He withdrew the key from the ignition and locked the car doors, then approached the colossal high school.

"You're late." The armed police officer stood in front of the walk-through metal detector, dividing the front entrance from the main corridor. "Go ahead and step through the checkpoint. I'll write up a disciplinary slip for your teacher."

"You *do* realize I'm the track champion of this entire school, don't you?" Brett stepped through the metal detector. "And waiting for that slip will just make me *more* late?"

"Give this to your teacher and proceed immediately to class." The police officer extended the yellow slip. "Don't get another one of these tomorrow, or you're suspended for two school days."

"So the punishment for not showing up to class on time two days in a row is getting kicked out of class two days in a row?"

Brett navigated through the labyrinthine hallways, passing countless lockers before approaching Ms. Lovelace's classroom.

"As we discussed earlier in the semester, *Hamlet* isn't a play so much as an obsession." Ms. Lovelace sat atop her desk, resting *The Complete Works of William Shakespeare* against her lap. "No sane playwright produces a work that takes four hours to perform, ends with all the major characters dying, and repeatedly compares sex with disease and damnation."

Brett walked to the back of the classroom and sat at the desk beside Julia.

"How thoughtful of you to join us today, Brett," Ms. Lovelace said. "Those of us who show up for this class on a *regular* basis have missed you."

"Things have been pretty out of control lately." He unzipped his backpack. "You know what it's like to have your hands full though, don't you, Ms. Lovelace?"

The class burst into laughter. The rumors had spread.

"As I was saying *before* our little interruption," Ms. Lovelace scowled, "Shakespeare wrote *Romeo and Juliet* years before *Hamlet,* but there's something bizarre about the chronological placement of *Romeo and Juliet* in Shakespeare's collected works. He wrote the play in the same period as his comedies such as *A Midsummer Night's Dream* and *Much Ado About Nothing,* and even though *Romeo and Juliet* opens as a comedy—with melodramatic professions of love and sexual innuendos—the story quickly spirals into a fable of crushed expectations and poisoned innocence."

"Hey Jules," Brett whispered. "Nice skirt. What's up in Jules Land?"

"Nothing." She kept her eyes focused on the front of the classroom.

"And it's not unintentional that Shakespeare's greatest love story opens with a brawl between two warring families, the Montagues and the Capulets," Ms. Lovelace continued. "However, one of the Montagues isn't interested in fighting, and instead spends his days mulling over his own heartbreak. 'She hath foresworn to love, and in that vow do I live dead that live to tell it now,' Romeo agonizes over Rosaline, the girl he wants. Of course, his cousins and friends ridicule him, only taking him seriously when he makes dirty jokes about his 'pump' and acts more interested in sex than love."

"Okay, Jules, how about this?" Brett sketched a stick figure in his notebook. "You have to draw a stick figure that kills my stick figure, and then I draw one that kills yours in a different way, and then you draw another one that kills mine in a totally different way. So if mine eradicates yours in a giant microwave, yours can drop a boulder on mine's head but can't eradicate him in a giant microwave."

"Brett, *please,*" Julia whispered. "Could you just *grow up* for *forty-five minutes?*"

"We're soon introduced to Juliet, a Capulet," Ms. Lovelace said. "She's engaged to the nobleman Paris at the behest of her family, but in the next scene—a Capulet ball that the Montagues have snuck into—Romeo and Juliet finally encounter each other. Even before speaking to Juliet, Romeo instantly forgets his heartbreak over Rosaline. 'Did my heart love till now?' he asks himself in act one, scene five. 'Foreswear it, sight! For I never saw true beauty till this night.' So what is Shakespeare suggesting here? That love at first sight exists? That Romeo and Juliet know they're destined for each other even before *speaking?* Or simply that hormone-crazed teenagers tend to base their sexual passions wholly on physical attractiveness?"

"Ms. Lovelace?" Julia raised her hand. "I'm really not sure Shakespeare would be saying that Romeo and Juliet are only into sex, because it seems like the whole point of the story is that all they have protecting them from the hateful world outside is love. And in the end it's obviously not enough since they both kill themselves, but if all they're doing the whole time is being controlled by their hormones then I'm not sure the play would have any real meaning behind it."

"Very good, Miss Ciardi." Ms. Lovelace smiled. "I'm growing more accustomed to having you in our class every time you raise your hand."

"Goody-goody," Brett muttered. "Won't even play the stick figure game."

"Listen, Brett, what is your *problem?* We're in *school* right now."

"God, are you all right? You seem really irritable this morning."

"Brett, I . . . I think we should just be friends, okay? I know that sounds really typical, but I can't hurt someone else like this and I know we're making Max so miserable and I don't want to hurt you either and I'm so tired of *hurting* people."

"Oh . . . that's cool, I guess." Brett gulped. "I mean, I thought we already decided to go ahead and be more than friends but . . . well . . . whatever, right?"

A knock came at the front door of the apartment. Max walked across the living room and opened the door. Trevor placed his arm around Max's shoulders, inviting himself into the apartment.

"Oh Christ, Max, I knew it. Fuck, man. . . . What happened?"

"I met this girl who moved in across the hall, and Brett *knew* I liked her, but that didn't stop him even though he could've had any other girl he'd wanted. I'm not even at school right now because it scares me to think about how much it's going to hurt to see them together."

"Holy shit, Max. You know, I'd always heard stories about how shitty Hunter treats you, but I never thought he'd actually do anything *that* fucking low."

"I just don't know about *anything* anymore. I couldn't get to sleep until like six in the morning and then I woke up at eight and I've had this sick feeling in my stomach all day like something really bad is going to happen soon."

"Hey man, you want to take the BMW over to my place? You can crash in the spare bedroom and we'll chill whenever you wake up."

"Okay . . . wow . . . you're a really nice guy for someone so famous and popular and rich and everything."

"You said you're into the Beatles, right? Check it out, you want to fly over to London next weekend and hang out with Paul McCartney?"

"What are you doing home so early, Dad?" Brett stepped into the kitchen and opened the refrigerator. "You're never home for lunch."

"That boy Thompson from your school came on the TV." Mr. Hunter sat at the dining room table. "Now *that's* a kid who's going somewhere, Brett. A kid this whole community can be proud of."

"You've never even *met* that egocentric asshole."

"We don't say derisive things about our local heroes in this household. What if the *neighbors* heard you say that? What would *they* think?"

"What are you talking about, Dad? Mr. and Mrs. Worthington across the street aren't spying on us, are they? Because I think they might be vampires."

"You have to keep up appearances for the neighborhood, Brett. That's something you'll learn as you grow older, but for now you should just try emulating Trevor Thompson. What harm could it do you in the long run?"

"Well, I like having a soul for one. And besides, do you really think Trevor Thompson on TV is the same Trevor Thompson in real life? I mean, Christ, the sportscaster on Channel Two makes me sound like fucking Gandhi whenever I win a race."

"Did you ever write that college application essay I told you to finish last week? It's due at the end of the month for early acceptance."

"Dad, I'm a *sophomore* in *high school.* Nobody starts worrying about college until junior year *at least,* unless they're an obsessive-compulsive psychopath."

"You can't get these scholarship applications in soon enough, Brett. Trust me, it's never too early to start planning your future."

"What if I don't care about my future?" Brett screamed. *"What if there* is *no future?"*

"Miss Lovelace?" Julia opened the classroom door. "Sorry for interrupting your lunch and everything. I was just wondering if maybe you have a second to talk?"

"Of course, Julia." Ms. Lovelace set her cup of yogurt on the desk. "What's on your mind?"

"Well, I . . . I guess I'm kind of in the middle of this situation, and I don't really know how to get out of it without hurting two other people. And the last thing in the world I want to do is hurt anybody, but I just don't know how to get *out.*"

"Does this have anything to do with Brett's absence yesterday and Max's today?"

"Oh God, I don't know how to make them be friends again and I don't know how to make them stop liking me so much, and I just wish they were both happy again like they were before I came here and ruined everything."

"Oh honey, don't say that. Besides, all Brett Hunter wants is sex, sex, sex."

"No, no, he's so much deeper than that, I know it. I've only been here for a few days, and I *know* there's so much goodness in him. But Max cares about me more than I know why and they both hate each other now, and I can't do anything *right* anymore and it's all my *fault.*"

"That's not true. No more tears, sweetie. Julia, do you have any idea how intelligent you are?"

"No . . ." she sniffled. "I don't think so."

"You've only been in my class for two days and I'm more impressed with you than any other student I've taught in years. If Brett and Max really care about you as much as you say, they'll both understand that you don't want to hurt either of them by choosing one over the other."

"Okay . . . if . . . if you say so." Julia wiped her cheeks with the backs of her shirt-sleeves. "I just hope it's not too late for everything to be okay again."

She said good-bye to Ms. Lovelace and stepped back into the hallway.

"Excuse me, young lady." The assistant principal stood against a row of lockers, holding a clipboard. "Your skirt may be a violation."

"Violation? Who . . . who are you?"

"On your knees, young lady. Now."

"I'm *sorry?* What's wrong with my skirt?"

"You know the drill. If that skirt doesn't touch the ground, it's an automatic deten-tion. On your *knees.*"

"I'm sorry, it's my second day here. At my old school we could wear whatever we wanted, so I didn't think it would be a violation."

"All right, you're coming with me."

"But I need to get to my next *class.*"

"Insubordination. Automatic detention."

"What? You can't. No, no, no, no, no."

"Hey man, you weren't in class this morning so I was just wondering what's . . . you know, what's going on and everything?"

"Brett? I thought I told you this cell phone is only for my parents in emergen-cies."

"Oh, right. Sorry about that. Listen, you want to hang out or anything after school? Maybe go skateboarding or whatever? You know . . . patch things up a little?"

"Actually I'm at Trevor's apartment right now. I was just about to go to sleep. Can I call you back later?"

"Trevor *Thompson?* You're at Trevor Thompson's *apartment* right now? What the fuck, Max? How do you know Trevor Thompson?"

"I didn't tell you he dropped by my place a couple days ago?"

"Dropped by your *place?* All right, whatever, Max. So do you want to hang out later or are the pod people going to be performing more experiments on your brain?"

"Actually I think I'm staying here for the big party tonight. Maybe we can go skateboarding tomorrow?"

"What the *fuck,* Max? Now *you're* too cool for *me?* Christ, it's bad enough that fucking asshole has to take my girl, now he's taking my best friend too?"

"I thought *Julia* is your girl, remember? And unless you forgot, *you're* the one who called off our friendship last night, not Trevor."

"You know what, Max? Fuck you, all right? Fuck you if you're not even going to let me try to make it up to you, because maybe I fucked up, but at least I'm *trying* to make things better and you're off partying with your new fucking in-crowd."

"Listen, Brett, I . . . I really have to go because I just can't deal with this anymore, okay? I'm tired of being your favorite loser to kick around, and now I've got a friend who treats me like I'm cool too. So we'll just talk tomorrow, all right?"

"You're out of your fucking league here, Max. These people aren't *like* you and me; do you understand that? They're vicious fucking animals, and the second you let yourself trust them they're going to tear you to pieces. Do you understand that, Max? Max? Max? Max—?"

"Brett, are you in there?" Mrs. Hunter opened the front door of the house and walked inside with two grocery bags. "You'll need to move your car out of the driveway before your father comes home. You know how crazy he gets."

"I'll do it later, all right?" Brett lay on the living room couch in front of the television. "How was work?"

"Not too bad. I picked up some groceries at the store, so why don't you put on some shoes and help carry the bags in from the car?"

"One minute. I'll do it after the commercial, okay?"

"You look like your grandmother, wrapped up in that old blanket. Why don't you put some clothes on and help carry in the groceries?"

"Mom, I think I'm going insane. Does that sound weird?"

"Oh honey, why would you say a thing like that? What's wrong?"

"Max is being bitchy and this girl from school dumped me and Quinn dumped me and Dad likes Trevor Thompson more than me and the only thing he ever does is scream and I can't deal with anything anymore and there's no control and I think I'm just getting ready to snap or go crazy or kill something or someone or kill my—"

"You're just having *teenage* feelings, Brett." Mrs. Hunter placed the bags onto the kitchen counter. "What you're going through is perfectly normal. It's probably just your hormones anyway."

"You're not even *listening* to me, Mom. I'm losing my fucking mind and you're not even *listening*."

"Oh . . . well then . . ." Mrs. Hunter tried to smile. "Maybe bringing in the groceries would help?"

−(RT/F) ln {[$P_K K^+_{in}$ + $P_{Na} Na^+_{in}$ + $P_{Cl} Cl_{out}$] & He knew that dreams are only the brain (%attempting to Interpret%) what had transpired the last eighteen hours but He could swear the reality of this cabin & these woods & the Pathway leading Him to the cliff overlooking the rocks & the lake & the two: children coming from the rocks to meet [$C_{30}H_{42}N_2O_2$ | $C^8H^{11}NO^2$] him & the little boy who talked while the girl smiled & stood in place & He fell to his knees / that they had come back to / forgive us / & He: "I . . . I don't understand . . . You're little kids now?" / "We're going to make everything okay, Maxwell!" / "We're little kids so we can be your friend again!" & the little girl held out [$C_{30}H_{42}N_2O_2$ | $C_8H_{11}NO_2$ | $C_{13}H_{16}N_2O_2$] the flower & smiled & placed it within his palm & the boy withdrew the blade from its sheathe & let it slide deep into HIS shoulder meat / & drank the gash: spraying into the [$P_K K^+_{out}$ + $P_{Na} Na^+_{out}$ + $P_{Cl} Cl_{-in}$] crimson lake HIS body now falling: sinking: breathing the blood-water & / the bottom ["Ashley?"] corpse with its mouthful of pills put Its hands around HIS neck: & pulled HIS naked body against Its & / Its hands across HIS chest & lower & [$C_{10}H_{12}N_2O$ | $C_{30}H_{42}N_2O_2$] "Fuck me?" It whispered with decomposing lips: & He wanted to swim back but the bleeding had stopped & It positioned him within Its hungry/spread/open Pathway: and It smiled as It rubbed against HIS—

"Max? Max? Wake up, little buddy! You're missing the fucking party!" Trevor grabbed onto Max's shoulders, shaking him into consciousness. "Come on, you've been asleep on that floor for ten hours now."

"All right, all right, I'm getting up." Max lifted his head from the pillow. "God, I was in the middle of the weirdest dream I've ever had in my life. . . . Where's the bathroom?"

"Right down the hallway." Trevor helped Max lift himself from the floor. "Hurry up, I want to introduce you to this supercute girl who doesn't have any guys working on her yet. And she's wearing *green*. You know what that means, right?"

"Oh, right, that was your whole thing about how all the girls wearing green want to—"

"Get fucked tonight for sure. The girls in yellow could go either way, which means they're just as fucking horny as the greens, but don't want to admit it. And the girls wearing red have boyfriends. Of course, we're not letting any of those frigid cunts inside tonight, so don't worry about getting shot down. After all, there's nothing like monogamy to spoil an otherwise perfect night."

"Okay . . . well, I think I'm going to go pee now, but maybe I can talk to that girl when I'm done?"

"She's waiting for you, Max. You need a condom? Or do you like to fuck your bitches commando style?"

"No thanks, Trevor." Max staggered into the hallway, passing numerous drunken and/or groping teenagers along the way. (Nearly all wore green or yellow clothing. One girl adorned herself in nothing but olive Pike & Crew thong panties.) The bathroom door burst open just as Max reached for the handle. The Star Quarterback stood naked in the doorway.

"No, it's not Trevor," Max said. "Are you okay?"

"Did we just hook up or sommmething? I thought I just hooked up with sommme-body."

"No . . . you . . . no . . . you didn't hook up with anyone tonight."

"That's good, I guess." A bead of saliva dripped down her chin, pooling onto the linoleum. "I don't *like* it when I forget hooking *up.*"

"Brett, are you awake?" Mr. Hunter opened the bedroom door. "Your mother wants to know if you're going to that movie with us tonight."

"Isn't it kind of late for you two to be going out?" Brett lay in the bed, his head stuffed between two pillows. "You wouldn't want to risk coming home after curfew, would you?"

"I can't figure it out, Brett. You insist on being so goddamn smart with your mouth all the time, but you still can't work your way up to a decent grade point average. I bring up college applications and you act like I'm the worst father in the world."

"Don't give yourself too much credit, Dad. There's still Woody Allen, right?"

"Why do you hate me so much, Brett? Sometimes I think about the first time I held you, right after the nurse washed you off in the delivery room, and I remember telling myself that I'd protect you and give you a good life. Now I ask myself every day what the hell I did wrong to make you give me all those looks of disgust and resentment."

"You scare the living shit out of me, Dad." Brett lifted his head from between the pillows. "You get so *angry* and make so many *demands* and always need to have it *your way* and never give me any freedom to make my own choices and you never stop comparing me to Trevor and my own brother and everyone else in the world who's better than me, and I just feel *strangled,* all right?"

"You're only sixteen years *old,* Brett. You don't even *know* how young that is because you think you're on top of the world now. My obligation as your father is to give you more and more slack as you get older, but still make sure that you're tied to the rope. Good Lord, Brett, I can't let you make *every* decision on your own. Is that what you *want?"*

Silence.

"Maybe I need to give you more opportunities to fall down on your own ass." Mr. Hunter sighed. "Because what we have now isn't *working.* What we have now isn't *normal* and it isn't *right* and it isn't *healthy* for anyone in this family, your mother included."

"Maybe you're right, Dad." Brett put his head back between the pillows. "Maybe I do need to be tied to a fucking rope."

*　　*　　*

"Holly, I'd like you to meet one of my closest friends, Max Brant." Trevor led Max to an auburn-haired girl drinking a Smirnoff Ice and sitting on the black leather sofa. "Max, this is Holly. You might recognize her from either her crowning at the homecoming dance or the Kapkovian Pacific cheerleading squad."

"Oh, I just started cheerleading this semester." She smiled. "It's a lot of fun, except for all the people who stereotype you as a bimbo who puts out for anyone."

"Oh Holly, high school boys can be so *immature*." Trevor shook his head and pinched Max's forearm. "Why can't they see that cheerleaders are passionate, motivated young women with *staggering* quantities of ambition and capacity?"

"Passionate." Max winced from the pinch. "Right."

"Like, I was going through the bookstore the other day." She twirled her hair. "You know, looking for Cliffs Notes for *Much Ado About Nothing* because I can't even get *through* that impossible-to-read shit. And this weird Jewish-looking kid was signing copies of some book called *Death to All Cheerleaders.* And it's just like, grow up and get a fucking *life,* you know?"

"Yeah . . . um . . . I hope that kid goes to Jew hell." Max turned to discover that Trevor had disappeared. "So . . . um . . . you're like a freshman or sophomore or—?"

"Junior." She crossed one leg over the other.

"So you're not a vegetarian or anything, are you?"

"No. Why would you think I'm a *vegetarian?*"

"I don't really know. Do you like the Beatles?"

"The *Beatles?* Whatever, I'm not into stuff that people made like fifty years ago. . . . Don't you listen to any *real* music? You know, like rap or something?"

"The Beatles broke up *thirty-three* years ago."

"Okay, Mr. Historian. So do you want to sit down?"

"Sure, I guess so." Max took a seat on the sofa. "So you're wearing green tonight?"

"Ummmm-hmmmm." She smiled. "What does the gray sweater mean?"

"I guess it means I forgot to wear green or yellow to the party. And I guess it means I like my gray sweater."

"You're a funny kid, Matt. So are you going to kiss me or just sit there staring at my tits all night?"

"No . . . I don't think so. Thanks anyway."

"What? You're *gay* or something?"

"No, no, no. It's just that you're not very interesting or nice or anything and you don't even remember my name, so I'm not sure anything we'd do would be very respectable since I don't really respect you at all."

"You fucking asshole." She bolted from the couch. *"Who the fuck do you think you are, you weird little shit? Why shouldn't I get the entire football team to smash your face right now?"*

"Could you please stop being so angry, Ms. Cheerleader?" Max covered his eyes and cowered against the black leather couch. "Sorry, I didn't mean it all *personally* or anything."

"It doesn't even matter anymore." Brett hunched in one corner of the darkened garage, using his mother's garden shears to split the yellow electrical cord dangling from the ceiling. "I'm never good enough for anyone and I'm tired of fighting against the fucking world and I'm just done trying because it doesn't even matter anymore."

He wrapped the cord around his forearm and lay against the cold concrete floor, sobbing into the soot and filth.

"So fucking pathetic." He wrapped the cord tighter and tighter around his arm. "I am so, so, so fucking pathetic right now."

Beeeeeeeep!

He lifted himself to his feet and picked up the telephone.

"Hey Brett, it's me."

"Oh, hey Jules. How . . . how are you?"

"Not so good, to be honest. I don't know, Brett, I've just been thinking about everything with you and me and Max all day and I really need someone to talk to, so can we maybe see each other tonight?"

"Okay . . . Actually I kind of need to finish something first, but if you want directions to my house or—"

"Sure, one second. Let me get a pencil, okay?"

"Jesus Christ, Max, what the hell did you say to piss Holly off so much?" Trevor laughed. "She just stormed out the front door screaming about how fucking hard it is to be perfect all the time."

"I . . . I don't know . . ." Max said. "I mean, I told her that I didn't want to screw around with her because she didn't seem very special or anything, and then she just sort of went totally crazy and said she'd get the football team to beat me up and I said I'm sorry, but she wouldn't stop pointing or shouting or—"

"You actually *said* that to her? Oh Christ, Max, you figured out the *secret?*"

"Um . . . I guess. . . . What secret?"

"That the easiest way to get in a girl's pants is to act like you don't care whether or not she catches on fire and fucking burns to death."

"Actually I was just being honest. When everyone just pretends they care about other people to get sex from them, how can anything real or special come out of that?"

"What? *Holly* isn't good enough for you? Come on, Max, I've heard of high standards, but you're *insane*. She's a fucking *stripper,* you know that, right?"

"Oh . . . I thought she said she's a junior? Don't you have to be eighteen to do that?"

"She had me find a guy in New York who prints fake IDs for fifty bucks. She makes eight hundred dollars a night now taking her panties off for dirty old men. Of course, I get special returns on my investment as often as I please. . . . Listen, Max, I think we both could use a drink right now, what do you think? Have you ever had scotch before?"

"Not really . . . You don't have any hard lemonade, do you?"

"*Lemonade?*" Trevor led Max through the horde of intoxicated/copulating teenagers. "Christ, Max, don't you think that's a little effeminate? Didn't Hunter ever teach you how to drink like a man?"

"Oh . . . sorry about that. Do you have any beer, I guess?"

"Let me check the fridge." Trevor opened the refrigerator door. *"Holy shit, all the Guinness is gone? What the fuck?"*

"Maybe people drank it or something?"

"All right, get your shit together. We're going on a beer run."

"Right now? Everybody's already here."

"This party is not going fucking dry before two in the morning." Trevor dragged Max across the apartment. "People come to these things to have *fun,* all right? And people can't *have* fun without *alcohol.* And if your party dries *out* before two in the *morning,* that reflects on your *reputation.* And your reputation is *everything,* because you're only as cool as your last fucking *party.* And if you can't see *that,* then maybe you should give up on ever being liked by anybody *other* than your mommy and—"

"Fuck you, Trevor." Brett stood in the doorway, soaked from the storm outside. "Where's Quinn?"

"Hunter?" Trevor grinned. "You always liked to come at unexpected times, didn't you? Although the last time, I remember it happened a little too early."

"Where is she, you insane son of a bitch?" Brett grabbed Trevor by the shirt collar and slammed him against the doorposts. *"Where the fuck is she?"*

"Settle down, Hunter. She's right here. You've found her."

"Why hasn't she called anyone since Saturday? Why do her parents think she ran away?"

"Quinn's been a little tied up lately, that's all." Trevor broke Brett's grip and walked back into the apartment. "You'll understand soon enough."

"Where do you fucking have her?" Brett followed Trevor through the sweltering throng of freak dancing couples in green and yellow. "Where?"

"Right here in the bedroom." Trevor led Brett down the shadowy hallway, past the girl adorned only in olive panties and a boy whose fingers writhed within. He unlocked the bedroom door with the master key. "You're going to absolutely love this, Hunter. Get ready for the biggest mind-fuck of your life."

He opened the door and let Brett inside, then slammed it and twisted the lock. Quinn's malnourished body lay strapped to the wooden bedposts: The Quarterback straddled her face and thrust his erection in and out of her unconscious lips, grabbing onto her semen-coated hair for leverage. White Mickey simultaneously thrust into Quinn's bleeding anus, insufficiently lubricated with KY Jelly. On the far side of the mattress, seven other boys waited in line for their turn at Quinn's vagina, mouth or rectum, all dripping with fresh globules of semen mixed into her own blood.

"Take her, Hunter." Trevor turned on his digital camcorder and began recording. "She's no more passed out than Ashley was when we fucked her together. She never *did* figure out which of us was the father, did she?"

Silence.

"You're *hesitating*, Hunter." Trevor circled the mattress, sliding a finger into Quinn's soft nest of pubic hair. The two boys continued thrusting into her chapped lips and blood-spattered anus. "Why are you *hesitating?* You're not actually *considering* it, are you? How many times have you thought about it? How many fucking times have you jerked off thinking about her spread open like that, just for you? *Take her,* Hunter. You know you want to do it, so go ahead and *fucking take her.*"

"You're dead, Trevor." Brett lunged across the bedroom. *"You are so motherfucking dead right now."*

The other boys knocked him to the ground, then kicked him repeatedly in the face and ribcage.

"What do you think *created* kids like us, Hunter?" Trevor removed Brett's shirt and unbuckled his leather belt, then laid him across Quinn's body. "I'd wager the feminist revolution myself." He snapped the belt across Brett's back. "Of course, nobody could argue *against* women getting equal pay for equal work, but what did America lose in the transition?" Another lashing. "Parents are never at home anymore because two paychecks need to be earned per household. The majority of married couples get divorced on a *whim*. Suddenly a woman's *independence* means *liberation from monogamy*. And as we both know, abortions are as easy to procure as a pair of new shoes." He snapped the belt down again. "Of *course* that was eventually going to trickle down to high schools. And what *spawned* that revolution? The Vietnam War. The death of our parents' innocence was the fucking abortion of ours. You and I are *products* of their war. We never even had a fucking *chance*."

Trevor rubbed Brett's bloody face against Quinn's vagina, inches from where White Mickey still thrust into her shredded anus.

"You broke the rules, Hunter. You actually started *caring* about her."

Silence.

"He told me everything, Brett. You actually left Ashley at the abortion clinic?"

"Left her at the clinic?" Brett coughed up blood. "Of *course* not. Christ, Max, I . . . listen, we both fucked her at the same time, all right? Every heterosexual combination you can possibly imagine. We didn't know which of us actually got her pregnant, and the DNA test didn't make any sense since she wanted an abortion anyway. So we just agreed to split the cost fifty-fifty—I'd put in three hundred and he'd put in three hundred—but then he never showed up with the money. Which is probably just pocket change for him anyway, right?"

"So why did he want to hurt you?"

"Well, that's kind of the funny thing. For some reason Trevor likes to take all these pictures of the girls he fucks, so he had me snap some digital pics of him and Ash, then he took some of Ash with me, and then we set the camera to go off automatically and took pictures of all three of us together."

"You made your own *porn?*"

"Well, I . . . I kind of . . . yeah, I kind of downloaded a couple of the pics onto my cell phone. When he wouldn't pay for the abortion, I mailed them express to his mom in this insane asylum in California."

"You're *kidding*, right? *You actually sent Trevor's mom pictures of you and him having sex with the same girl?*"

"Good Lord, is that royally fucked-up or what?" Brett doubled up on the floor laughing. "Oh my God, I think that's the most brilliant thing I've ever done."

"So is that why he started dating Quinn? To get back at you?"

"I don't even *know* what kind of morbid shit goes through his mind. . . . It's over for good though. I'm exiling myself from the kingdom."

"What do you mean it's all over? What about Julia?"

"We're just going to be friends now, all right? For you."

"Oh . . . I'm really sorry that I said I hated you."

"You know I never corrupted her, don't you? It was never about the sex, you have to believe that. We dated for two days and only kissed on the lips *once.* Christ, Max, I've fucked thirty-seven girls—three in one *day* last summer—and I've never loved a single one of them. Julia was different."

"What about Quinn? You didn't love her?"

"The first time we had sex, I actually said that to her. She just told me that teenagers always think they're in love, but never really are because it's only chemical reactions inside our brains . . . Listen, Max, sex doesn't mean *anything,* all right? That's what I tried to explain to you after you slept with Ashley the other night, but you wouldn't listen. It doesn't *matter* whether everybody fucks everyone else—and it doesn't even matter whether they remember each other's names, because the real problem *isn't* people hooking up. The problem is that everyone wants to be loved deep down, but nobody even thinks it *exists* anymore. You remember how I used to wear Bad Religion T-shirts and talk shit about everyone who wore Pike & Crew? Well, I found out that girls only get with you if you wear those labels on your chest. And in ten years, nobody will be wearing Pike & Crew—it'll just be some *other* label that helps kids give up everything that makes them special, because people are so afraid of themselves."

"Seriously, Brett, are you okay?" Max asked. "You look kind of crazy right now."

"You know what's really fucked-up, man? When my brother went off to college he had to leave his girlfriend back home, right? And they decided to stay together until he came back for winter vacation, except halfway through the semester she called and told him she wanted an open relationship. The first time he saw her after coming back—at some New Year's party on Hillside—she actually fucked this twenty-seven-year-old guy on his own grandmother's bed. She hadn't even met him before that night. So my brother drove to the Point and kept going till he went off the fucking edge and broke every bone in his body. The newspapers and TV stations said they wouldn't report it because that might encourage other people to commit suicide, and my parents never talk about it and neither do I and he's still in a coma down at the same hospital where Ashley's going insane and I'm not sure but I think I'm starting to feel like he must've when he left that fucking New Year's party."

"What are you talking about, Brett? Your brother is—"

"What do you say?" Brett staggered to his feet and limped shirtless to the elevator. "One last drive?"

"One second, all right?" Max opened the apartment door. "I think I left my sweater on the couch."

When he returned, Brett was gone.

"Where do you think *you're* going, little buddy?" Trevor clamped a hand down on Max's shoulder. "You weren't granted permission to leave."

"You beat the shit out of Brett," Max said. *"You hurt my best friend."*

"You're so out of the fucking loop, Brant. We're still going on our little drive."

"You hurt Brett, Trevor. I'm not going anywhere with you."

"Surely Hunter told you what transpired in that bedroom." Trevor grabbed Max's earlobe and pulled him into the elevator. "You're going to be neutralized."

"Neutralized? What do you *mean?* Oh God, where'd Brett go?"

The elevator doors opened inside the subterranean parking garage. Trevor pulled Max across the garage and unlocked the BMW.

"We're going to meet a special friend of mine," Trevor said. "And then you'll get to go back home."

"You're not going to hurt me, are you? You're not going to *kill* me, are you?"

Trevor shoved Max into the passenger seat, then took his own place behind the steering wheel.

"You're more like Hunter than you even know, Brant." Trevor backed the BMW out of the garage. "Of course, he knows how to talk girls into swallowing his cum on a daily basis, but deep down you're both too pussy to take what you want when it's right there waiting for you."

"*You don't even know Brett deep down.* You've only had *sex* with the same *girl* as him and so have *I* and you don't know me either *so just stop talking.*"

"Christ, Max, I'm not going to kill you." Trevor steered the BMW onto the water-logged street. "I'm simply going to hold a razorblade to your throat and force you to ingest a vial of Gamma Hydroxybutyrate. You'll be rendered unconscious for eight or ten hours and won't remember anything. Otherwise you'll be fine when you wake up in the morning."

"Could you maybe slow the car down a little bit?" Max tried to open the passenger side door. "You're going over the speed limit."

"Safety locks, Max. They don't open while the automobile is in motion." Trevor accelerated the BMW wildly through the crashing rain. "You didn't really want to hit the pavement at this speed anyway, did you?"

"No . . . " Max started to cry.

"This special friend and I have an interesting arrangement." Trevor smirked. "He supplies me with GHB and in return I make photographs and videos of underage girls getting fucked and bloodied in every orifice. He sells these images to perverts world-wide on the Internet and we split the profits fifty-fifty. Of course, you're not going to remember that in fifteen minutes, so there's no harm in letting you in on the secret, is there?"

"Why do you even need the drug in the first place? Why can't you just have sex with sober girls? Wouldn't Quinn have slept with you anyway?"

"Oh my God, Max, does it even fucking *matter?*" Trevor laughed. "That's the *best fucking part* with these stupid high school bitches. You said you fucked Ashley, didn't you? Yes? Well, *she* wasn't fucking sober when you put it in her sloppy cunt, *was* she?"

"I . . . I was drunk too, if that makes any difference."

"You had her at your fucking *mercy*, Max. She was completely *vulnerable* and you took *advantage* of that simply because you *wanted* to. You conquered her in the most humiliating way *possible*—and you know you got off on *every fucking second of it.*"

"*That's not how it happened, Trevor. That's not how it happened.*"

"You know you loved having her like that, Max, so don't pretend that lying to me changes anything. And in all honesty, I'm only a slight amplification away from you and Hunter and everyone else who's ever fucked a whore like Ashley Iverson."

"Jesus, Trevor. Slow down." Max gripped onto the leather armrest as the BMW hurtled toward a four-way intersection at ninety miles per hour. "You're *sober* now, right? I mean, sober enough to drive and everything?"

"Relax, Brant. It's easy if you don't get paranoid."

The streetlight turned to red.

"Yes . . . ? Can . . . can I help you, young lady?" Mrs. Hunter opened the front door of the house, fingers trembling. "Isn't it a bit late to be knocking door to door? In this weather especially?"

"Oh, I'm so sorry. Is Brett home?" Julia looked from Mrs. Hunter to the white ambulance and five police cars parked in the driveway. "Or—?"

"You stupid fucking psychotic *asshole.*" Max leaned against the smoking, demolished BMW and pinched his nose to stop the bleeding. "What, you didn't *notice* the SUV heading *straight for us?* You didn't *notice* you were going *ninety miles per hour through a yellow light?*"

"Yes! I fucking *know* that, you obvious little shit." Trevor fell to the pavement and covered his rain-soaked face with both hands. "At least we're still *alive,* Brant. At least we're not *killed* or *paralyzed* or . . . where do you think *you're* going?"

"Home, Trevor. Good luck not getting arrested by the fucking cops."

"Oh God, it won't hurt." Julia sat atop the steel guardrail of the apartment complex's rooftop. "It'll just take a few seconds and then I can die and if there's a God I can be with Brett again and if there isn't that's okay too, because I can still be dead and it'll just take a few seconds and it probably won't even hurt and if it does I don't care because I made Brett die and I deserve it and I'm so sorry God I'm so sorry I'm so so so so so so sorry."

An orange taxi pulled to the curbside down below.

"Max . . . ? Is . . . is that . . . ? *Max! Max! Up here! On the roof!*"

"Julia? Why are you sitting on the edge?" Max stepped out of the taxi with visible agony and handed the driver a twenty-dollar bill. "Stay still, all right? I'll be right there."

He reached the rooftop ten minutes later, limping halfway to the guardrail before succumbing to exhaustion. Julia stepped down from the edge and cradled him.

"Listen, I was wrong, okay?" Max whispered. "If Brett's the one who makes you happy, then that makes me happy too. And I'm sorry for making you choose and I'm sorry I said I hated him because I really don't and I just want everything to be okay again like it was before."

"Oh God, Max, please stop talking." She tried to breathe through her sobs. "Do you know adults call it teen angst? When we fall in love and get our hearts broken or don't like the way the world is or aren't sure how to be ourselves anymore, they call it teen angst because they want to pretend it didn't hurt to grow up. They don't want to remember, so they call it teen angst and make themselves cold to life and forget that it hurts *so, so much,* and for some people it just hurts too much. For some people it just breaks them."

"Julia? What's . . . what's wrong?"

"Hold me, Max. I'll tell you."

↗ S.L.U.T.STATS

63%:

Percentage of teenage suicides in which the victim lives in a single-parent home
[Source: Federal Bureau of Investigation]

500,000:

Number of American teenagers who attempt suicide per year
[Source: Columbia University]

8%:

Percentage of teenagers who attempt suicide annually
[Source: The U.S. Centers for Disease Control and Prevention]

90%:

Percentage of parents who believe they could see the warning signs of suicide if their teenager were suicidal
[Source: *The Washington Post*/Positive Action for Teen Health]

American 15- to 24-year-olds who committed suicide in 1999: **3,901**
Living Americans who have attempted suicide at least once: **5,000,000**
Fastest-growing age group for attempted/completed suicide: **10 to 14-year-olds**
[Source: The American Association of Suicidology]

"Jacksonville, FL—Four boys were arrested Monday, accused of
sexual battery on a girl at a middle school in Northwest
Jacksonville. Police say a 12-year-old student at Eugene Butler
Middle School was late for class and was heading to the office
to get a pass when she was pulled into the bathroom by one of
the boys. She said one boy raped her and three others forced her
to perform oral sex. . . . According to police, two of the boys
are 12 years old, one is 13 and the other is 14. Because of
their ages, their names were not released. Police say the boys
admit their roles in the attack."
—WKMG-TV (A WASHINGTON POST COMPANY), APRIL 2, 2003

"LOS ANGELES—Three high school classmates accused of sexually
assaulting a UCLA student during a school-arranged campus tour
have pleaded innocent to rape charges. The teenagers, from Carson
High School, just south of Los Angeles, were touring campus with
several other students and a counselor December 5 when they left
the group and allegedly attacked the University of California,
Los Angeles, student in a dormitory, authorities said. The two
17-year-olds and a 16-year-old were ordered held Friday in juvenile custody pending a December 26 hearing. . . . One of the 17-
year-olds also pleaded innocent to sexual battery for allegedly
attacking another dormitory resident the same day."
—THE ASSOCIATED PRESS, DECEMBER 14, 2002

"Who can blame us for being paranoid and dead inside? It's easier
just to try not to have a soul. I've never been in love. I've pro-
tected myself from one kind of pain while becoming susceptible to
another."
—AMY T., 19, ANNAPOLIS, MARYLAND

"The Bethesda subdivision of $600,000 townhouses and leafy courtyards is a tranquil counterpoint to the brutality alleged to have occurred there this month: the sexual assault of an 'adult entertainer' by three Walt Whitman High School students who police said lured her to the house with an offer to make an adult video. Montgomery County police said the three students—ages 14, 15 and 19—skipped class on the morning of November 8 and lured a 25-year-old woman from an escort service to one of the students' homes in Bethesda. When the woman arrived, they beat her with a baseball bat, attempted to cover her mouth with a cloth that emitted a 'medicinal odor,' then sexually assaulted her with the bat and another object, police said. Police said the students got the woman's number from an Internet ad and told her they were adult video producers who wanted to offer her a job."
—THE WASHINGTON POST, NOVEMBER 17, 2002

"New Orleans—Gunmen armed with an AK-47 rifle and a handgun opened fire in a packed high school gym today, killing a 15-year-old youth and wounding three teenage girls in a spray of more than 30 bullets that sent students scrambling for cover. Four suspects, ranging in age from 15 to 19, were arrested in a sweep of the neighborhood near John McDonogh Senior High School."
—THE ASSOCIATED PRESS, APRIL 15, 2003

"A 12-year-old Rockville girl was charged as a juvenile yesterday in the fatal stabbing of her 15-year-old brother, who was killed after the siblings argued over whose turn it was to use the telephone, law enforcement sources said. The girl stabbed her brother in the heart with a steak knife Thursday night, the sources said."
—THE WASHINGTON POST, MARCH 8, 2003

"Walker, MN—Two 16-year-old boys charged with killing a blind man in Minnesota might have been drunk when they allegedly beat him with an ax handle, authorities said. . . . [The man] was pronounced dead at a hospital. His head was severely cut and bruised, back and front, a criminal complaint said."
—THE ASSOCIATED PRESS, DECEMBER 3, 2002

"Riverside, CA—Two young men killed their mother and tried to cover their tracks by chopping off her head and hands the way they saw it done on [television program] The Sopranos, authorities said Monday. Jason Bautista, 20, and his 15-year-old half brother, who was not identified because of his age, were arrested over the weekend for investigation of murder, Sheriff Michael Carona said. . . . 'I don't know what motive you could possibly give for killing your mother,' Carona said."
—THE ASSOCIATED PRESS, JANUARY 27, 2003

"What began as several teenagers [aged 13 to 14] tormenting a mentally retarded man in the lobby of his Hartford apartment building Saturday afternoon escalated into an attack that left him dead, according to two men who viewed a videotape of the incident. One teen flung a full bottle of soda against Ricky Whistnant's head so hard the 39-year-old man fell over sideways, hitting the other side of his head against a wall as he collapsed, said the men who watched the surveillance camera videotape. The teens then surrounded Whistnant, kicking him and opening more soda bottles to pour over his motionless body, according to [the] superintendent of the building and the assistant manager."
—THE HARTFORD COURANT, APRIL 7, 2003

"Pensacola, FL—Two Florida brothers will serve sentences in state prison after pleading guilty to killing their father with a baseball bat, a judge announced Thursday. Derek King, 14, will spend eight years in state prison, and his 13-year-old brother Alex will spend seven years in state prison. . . . In a statement signed as part of his pleading, Derek King, 14, admitted killing his father at the suggestion of his 13-year-old brother. 'I murdered my dad with an aluminum baseball bat and I set the house on fire from my dad's bedroom,' Derek said in the statement."
—CNN, NOVEMBER 14, 2002

"Charlotte, NC—On New Year's Day 1999, a 30-year-old disabled
man, Edward Henry Mingo, was stabbed repeatedly in the chest and
back, his head beaten with a hammer. A week later, police made
another disturbing revelation: A 14-year-old and a 15-year-old
were charged. . . . The slaying shocked the two hundred residents
at the high-rise on West Tenth Street, a public housing complex
for the elderly and disabled."
—THE CHARLOTTE OBSERVER, JUNE 27, 2000

"Lake Worth, FL—Police say the 13-year-old boy suspected in the
fatal shooting of a teacher at a Florida middle school told a
classmate that day that he would 'be all over the news.' But the
parents of seventh-grade honor roll student Nathaniel Brazill
believe the death of teacher Barry Grunow on May 26 was an accident. 'He loved Mr. Grunow. They were best friends,' said the boy's
mother, Polly Powell. 'You just don't shoot your best friends.'"
—CNN, MAY 4, 2001

"Ellicott City, MD—A teenager was charged Thursday with first-
degree murder for allegedly killing a romantic rival by spiking
his soda with cyanide. Police said Ryan Furlough, 18, laced his
friend's drink with the poison as they played video games in
Furlough's basement in Ellicott City in suburban Baltimore."
—THE ASSOCIATED PRESS, JANUARY 9, 2002

"Philadelphia, MS—A Circuit Court jury found 17-year-old Luke
Woodham guilty Friday of murder in the death of his mother last
fall. Prosecutors accused the teen of stabbing and beating fifty-
year-old Mary Woodham on October 1, then going on a rampage at
Pearl High School, where he unleashed a hail of gunfire that killed
two classmates and injured seven others. . . . A tearful Woodham
testified Thursday that he didn't recall slashing his mother to
death with a butcher knife. . . . 'I just closed my eyes and fought
with myself because I didn't want to do any of it,' he said. 'When
I opened my eyes, my mother was lying in her bed dead.'"
—CNN, JUNE 5, 1998

"Bartow, FL—The fate of a 15-year-old boy accused of killing his 8-year-old neighbor—then stuffing her body under his bed—landed in the hands of a jury on Thursday, after his attorney made a last-ditch plea for the panel to find the teen guilty of manslaughter. . . . Prosecutor Harry Shorstein said the boy was guilty of 'three vicious attacks' in which he hit the girl with a baseball bat, cut her throat and then repeatedly stabbed her before hiding her body beneath his waterbed in his parents' Jacksonville, FL, home on November 3, 1998."
—CNN, JULY 8, 1999

"Tom's River, NJ—A teenager was sentenced Friday to life in prison for carjacking and killing a teacher, who managed to secretly record the attack and her desperate pleas to be spared. Michael LaSane, 17, will not be eligible for parole for 30 years. He pleaded January 27 to felony murder in the death of Kathleen Weinstein, 45. . . . LaSane said he bound her ankles and wrists with duct tape and . . . smothered her after fearing a nearby utility crew could hear her screaming. Before she was killed, Weinstein managed to activate a small, concealed tape recorder. It recorded a 46-minute conversation in which Weinstein could be heard crying, begging for her life and warning her attacker of the trouble he would face if he did not spare her."
—CNN, FEBRUARY 28, 1997

A LETTER TO ANDY WILLIAMS, FIFTEEN-YEAR-OLD MURDERER

"I don't care if I die in the shootout, all I want is to kill and injure as many of you pussies as I can. . . . You all better fucking hide in your houses because I'm coming for EVERYONE soon, and I WILL be armed to the fucking teeth and I WILL shoot to kill and I WILL FUCKING KILL EVERYTHING. . . . You people had my phone #, and I asked and all, but no no no no no don't let the weird-looking Eric kid come along. . . . I am the law, and if you don't like it, you die. If I don't like you or I don't like what you want me to do, you die. . . . Feel no remorse, no sense of shame."

—FROM THE JOURNALS OF EIGHTEEN-YEAR-OLD ERIC HARRIS, DAYS BEFORE HE AND SEVENTEEN-YEAR-OLD DYLAN KLEBOLD KILLED TWELVE CLASSMATES, ONE TEACHER AND THEMSELVES IN THE LIBRARY OF LITTLETON, COLORADO'S COLUMBINE HIGH SCHOOL ON APRIL 20, 1999

"Columbine is a clean, good place, except for those rejects. . . . Sure, we teased them. But what do you expect with kids who come to school with weird hairdos and horns on their hats? It's not just jocks; the whole school's disgusted with them. They're a bunch of homos. . . . If you want to get rid of someone, usually you tease 'em. So the whole school would call them homos."

—EVAN TODD, 255-POUND LINEBACKER FOR THE COLUMBINE FOOTBALL TEAM, IN A DECEMBER 20, 1999, TIME MAGAZINE INTERVIEW

March 11, 2001

They called you a faggot, Andy. They put cigarettes out on the back of your neck. They stole and broke the skateboard your dad gave you for your fifteenth birthday. They kicked you behind Dumpsters until you confessed to being their bitch. They whipped you with wet towels in the locker room and welted your body. They forced you to pick up their drugs, "because if you get caught, you're nobody." They beat the living shit out of you every day—sometimes smashing you face-first into a tree—and took your lunch money. Once, they held you down, soaked your clothes with hairspray, and set you ablaze with a Zippo. And of course they told you that if you didn't fight back you'd be "a bitch and a pussy," so what the hell, Andy:

"Santee, CA—A fifteen-year-old boy who had been picked on and had talked about shooting classmates allegedly opened fire in a high school bathroom, killing two people and wounding 13 in the deadliest U.S. school attack since Columbine. One student said the boy, a freshman, had a smile on his face as he fired away with a pistol at Santana High School in this middle-class San Diego suburb. The student surrendered in the bathroom, dropped his gun and said he acted alone, telling officers: 'It's just me.' according to sheriff's officials. . . . The slain students were identified as Bryan Zuckor, 14, and Randy Gordon, 15."
—THE ASSOCIATED PRESS, MARCH 6, 2001

You fired nearly thirty shots in all, police said, leaving two boys dead and a dozen more in the hospital, along with one school security guard. Your friends and family never saw it coming, even though you gave them ample warning.

NEIL O'GRADY, 15, to the *New York Times:* "He was telling us how he was going to bring a gun to school . . . but we thought he was joking. We were like, 'Yeah, right.'"

JOSHUA STEVENS, 15, to the *New York Times:* "He had it all planned out, but at the end of the weekend he said he was just joking and he wasn't really going to do it. I said, 'Like, you better be.' And he said, 'No, I'm serious.'"

Your father, divorced from your mother for most of your life, was distraught. "Mere words cannot express the remorse I feel for the families," he said, choking back tears at a press conference. "I would like to express my sympathy and sorrow to all those affected."

Reporters hassled your mother at home. She wept from behind her front door: "He's lost. His future is gone."

Your future as a normal teenage boy, anyway. On the other hand, your future as the media's newest Christ figure for angry, ostracized suburban teenagers is looking pretty decent right now:

"For the next few days, the nation will once again stare at the photograph of a slight, confused-looking teenage boy, trying to understand the unfathomable—how Charles Andrew Williams, age 15, could open fire on his classmates, killing two and wounding 13 other people. We'll stare at those pictures as the explanations begin to pour in from the experts and the pundits alike. We'll hear from psychologists who'll draw elaborate profiles of misfits and loners, of adolescent depression and acting out."
—NEWSDAY, MARCH 8, 2001

"Because he has refocused national attention on the sullen, confused kids who skulk around our schools, harboring grudges and entertaining violent demons, and has forced us to ask sickeningly familiar, unflattering questions about our country and our societal obsession with violence, Charles 'Andy' Williams is our person of the week. . . . When he appeared in court Wednesday, he was alone—neither his mother, who lives in South Carolina, nor his father attended the hearing. This kid, it is clear, is operating utterly without the safety net called family."
—TIME MAGAZINE, MARCH 9, 2001

And that's what's so fascinating about you, Andy: You're a pipsqueak and a loser and your life probably sucked from the get-go, but *you're not crazy*. Now, Eric Harris and Dylan Klebold, *they* were fucking crazy.

"Kill mankind," Harris wrote in his journal months before the Columbine massacre, cheerfully adding, "No one should survive," and "After I mow down a whole area full of you snotty-ass rich motherfucker high-strung God-like-attitude-having worthless pieces of shit whores, I don't care if I live or die."

But you're different, Andy: You're just a little kid who got pushed too far and had the means to retaliate. You're just a little kid who got turned into a fucking animal.

JESSICA MOORE, 15, to the Associated Press: "He was picked on all the time. He was picked on because he was one of the scrawniest guys. People called him freak, dork, nerd—stuff like that."

NEIL O'GRADY to the Associated Press: "People think he's dumb."

Your community is hurting now, Andy. Both of your victims had hopes and dreams: Gordon would've enlisted in the U.S. Navy after graduation, and Zuckor wanted to either attend medical school or become a Hollywood stuntman.

"A stuntman or a doctor," remarked Santana High School Principal Karen Degischer at Zuckor's funeral. "What a beauty of youth that one could think that you could be one or the other, maybe even both."

So did you get your revenge, Andy? Did you give Santee, California, what it had coming?

"He was an angry young man," said San Diego County District Attorney Paul Pfingst soon after your arrest. "I don't know at who or what. He was just a mad young man."

Of course, what Pfingst most likely wouldn't understand is that there's a hell of a lot to be angry about as an American teenager today: Our generation is one that values appearance, athletic accomplishment and sexual conquest far more than anything of substance, and those of us who don't conform to the standard mold are routinely excluded and mocked for our deviation. But anger, even when justified, *must* be controlled and channeled, Andy, or else it inevitably becomes insane, hollow vengeance. Or else—to state the obvious—it inevitably becomes *you*.

JOHN SCHARDT, 17, to the Associated Press: "I looked at the kid and he was smiling and shooting his weapon. People were trying to take cover. It was total chaos."

SHANNON DURRETT, 15, to the Associated Press: "I never thought Andy would do this. He liked skateboarding and hung out with his skateboarding friends. . . . He was nice, he was funny; someone who would never *do* something like this."

Andy, it's possible that you went to school with your father's gun last Monday to make a statement for all the little guys who get teased and ridiculed and beaten for everything they do. Hell, maybe you even believed in your heart of hearts that every last teen outcast would be better off if you just proved once and for all that it's possible to push the kids who can't dance too far. But the truth is you've only made people even *more* scared of high school outsiders, and further persecution will unavoidably result. You're no savior, Charles Andrew Williams: You're simply a pathetic murderer, and this eighteen-year-old for one cannot find it in himself to pity you.

Sincerly,
Marty Beckerman

"El Cajon, CA—The teen who killed two students and wounded 13 others at a high school last year was sentenced Thursday to 50 years to life in prison after he tearfully apologized for the shooting rampage. Charles 'Andy' Williams didn't explain why he opened fire with his father's handgun at Santana High School in Santee on March 5, 2001, but said he felt 'horrible about what happened. . . . If I could go back to that day, I would never have gotten out of bed,' the 16-year-old said, his voice breaking."

—THE ASSOCIATED PRESS, AUGUST 15, 2002

"Houston—A teacher at a Pasadena private school charged with sexually assaulting a 13-year-old boy appeared Monday in a Houston courtroom. Investigators told News2Houston that Lisa Zuniga, 27, had sex with a student and that she may be six months pregnant with his baby. . . . Zuniga worked at the Victory Academy for two years. It is a private church school that teaches an accelerated Christian education program. 'The 13-year-old is a child (and) he cannot give consent,' Sgt. Tim Moon said. 'I just imagine he was seduced by this older woman. She took advantage of him.'"

—MSNBC, NOVEMBER 4, 2002

"A former student has testified that a high school band teacher
performed a sexual act on her on two separate occasions. John Perry
Dornbusch of Hidalgo [TX] is charged with three counts of sexual
performance on a child for incidents involving two girls. He faces
a maximum sentence of 20 years in prison and a $10,000 fine. The
19-year-old woman, who was not identified, testified Thursday that
Dornsbusch took her and another girl to a motel room in December
2000. She said Dornbusch went to a bed with her friend, then later
performed oral sex on her. The woman also says Dornbusch performed
oral sex on her in a storage room in July 2000."
—THE ASSOCIATED PRESS, JULY 27, 2002

"Kent, WA—A former teacher who had sex with a sixth-grade
student and later gave birth to his child was sentenced Friday
to six months in jail. Mary Kay LeTourneau, 35, who pleaded
guilty in August to two counts of second-degree child rape,
has already served 100 days of that sentence while awaiting
trial. . . . 'Please help me,' she said. 'Help us all.'"
—CNN, NOVEMBER 14, 1997

WEDNESDAY

↗ WEDNESDAY

Good morning, this is a News Six special report. Seventeen-year-old Kapkovian Pacific Secondary School student and prominent local author Trevor Thompson was arrested late last night on charges of drunk driving, kidnapping, possession of a controlled substance, conspiracy to commit forced sodomy and manufacturing of child pornography with the intent to distribute. Authorities said Thompson was arrested shortly after an automobile accident caused when his 2003 BMW crossed an intersection at nearly ninety miles per hour. According to police sources, Thompson's blood-alcohol level exceeded the legal limit, and a search of his downtown apartment found more than eighty-five Kapkovian Pacific students throwing an alcohol-fueled party inside. Authorities also discovered nine male students forcing intercourse on an unconscious sixteen-year-old girl—a sophomore at Kapkovian Pacific—who was immediately taken to Grace Alliance Medical Center for treatment. Those nine students—who range in age between fourteen and eighteen—are now in police custody. Thompson remains at the Municipal Pretrial Facility until his arraignment this afternoon. His bail is set at nearly one and a half million dollars, an estimated ninety percent of his total assets. When News Six contacted Thompson's publisher, a spokesperson explained that Thompson's multibook contract had already been terminated. Calls to Thompson's literary agent were not immediately returned as of press time. Thompson's father, an executive at AOL-Time Warner in New York, released a statement expressing his sympathy for the sixteen-year-old girl and her family. Thompson's mother, who resides in an assisted-living facility in Oceanside, California, could not be reached for comment. The sixteen-year-old sexual assault victim is currently listed in stable condition at Grace Alliance, although a twenty-year-old also found unconscious at the party is still in critical condition. Neither Kapkovian Pacific administrators nor school district officials will comment on the matter at this time. This has been a News Six special report. News Six: Your leader for local news.

"Can I help you, young man?" the Youth Ward Receptionist asked. "Visiting hours aren't until noon."

"Oh . . ." Max extended a crumpled ten-dollar bill from his pocket. "Ashley Iverson?"

"Keep your lunch money." The receptionist sighed and opened the inpatient directory on her desk. "If it's that important for you to . . . hmm . . . sir, I'm not seeing anyone under. . . . oh . . . oh, dear."

"What is it? What's wrong?"

"Transferred to the Intensive Care Unit. She must have relapsed like those others last night. What a shame. You can't visit anyone in ICU unless you're direct family. In any case, she might've already been transferred to Recovery, God willing."

"Can you visit people in Recovery?"

"Take one of those little maps off the wall. I'll show you how to get there."

Max took the elevator down two flights and crossed the sky bridge to the Recovery Ward. The receptionist there faced the wall, entering data into a computer. Max passed into the corridor and looked through each doorway.

"Who . . . who are you?" Ashley lay supine, strapped to the hospital mattress, a steel bedpan by her side.

"Oh . . . I'm . . . I'm Max Brant. We kind of hooked up Friday night. . . . I don't know if you remember it that well."

"What happened to my friends? The doctors come and give me the happy pills, but they won't tell me what happened. Are they dead? Did they die? Did they *die?*"

"I . . . I don't know. What are you talking about?"

"They were my *friends.* They got the slushies."

"Listen, Ashley, ever since . . . ever since Brett told me what happened with your mom's pills I've been wondering if it's my fault or not, and I know it's rude to ask, but please tell me why you wanted out so I can stop hating myself."

"Why I wanted out? That's what Brett asked. Why? Why? Why? Doesn't anybody *get* it? I'm just *sad,* okay? I don't fucking know who I am and sometimes I think I do when I'm wearing Pike & Crew, but I'm just *sad* and *scared* and *alone,* all right?"

"Oh . . . so it's . . . it's not because of Friday night?"

"Oh God, I don't even *remember* Friday night. You actually think I tried to *kill myself* because we *hooked up?* What's *wrong* with you? *Who are you? Why are you here?*"

"I'll leave now, okay?" Max stepped toward the door. "I'm sorry I did the wrong thing and I'm sorry I took advantage of you and I'm sorry even though you don't remember because it was the wrong thing and I don't ever want to be like Trevor."

"Go away," Ashley cried, unable to move her hands to wipe away the tears. "Just go away and let me die."

Max walked back into the corridor and approached the elevator, then stopped as soon as he realized who occupied the last bedroom.

"*Max?*" Quinn lay on the mattress, an intravenous tube extending from her arm. "What are *you* doing here?"

"*Quinn?* Are you *okay?*"

"Yeah . . . The doctors said I should be able to walk by tomorrow . . . and they gave me some painkillers so it . . . it doesn't hurt so much to . . ."

Silence.

"Why did he do it, Max? Why did he fucking do it?"

"I . . . I don't know. . . . Brett said something about being an exile from the kingdom, but I don't know what that means and I'm . . . I'm the last person he ever talked to."

"Oh God, what was I *thinking?* Why didn't I just stay *together* with him? Then he'd still be alive and I wouldn't be in this hospital and Trevor would've found some other girl to fucking torture. I mean, I wanted an open relationship so I could have *fun* with other guys or whatever and not have to *worry* about any deep emotional stuff and just be a *sixteen-year-old girl,* you know? So I went to prom with Trevor and five days later Brett's *dead* and do you think that's a *coincidence?* Oh God, I thought I could just go back to him if I ever wanted anything serious, and now I'm never going to *talk* to him again. *Nobody is ever going to talk to him again.*"

Silence.

"I used to cut myself, did he ever tell you that?" Quinn said. "The first time I was six years old. My parents were fighting about getting divorced so I went to the kitchen and got a knife and just started slashing everywhere. And they stopped fighting to take me to the hospital, and it just made me so happy that they were finally paying attention to me. So I'd do it every time they pissed me off, until Brett told me to stop because it hurt him to see me like that, but now he's *dead* and I don't even *know* what I'm going to do to myself . . . I don't even think I want to go to the funeral. It's too fucked-up for me to go to something like that when it's my fault in the first place."

"You shouldn't think that," Max said. "Maybe he didn't do it sooner because we were in his life."

"Whatever." She laid her head against the pillowcase. "Oh God, I just miss how good things used to be."

"Please don't do anything to yourself, Quinn." Max turned back toward the corridor. "One is enough forever."

He took the elevator down to the hospital lobby and withdrew his skateboard from beneath one of the leather couches, then exited through the automatic sliding doors. The ride to Brett's house was downhill all the way.

"Oh Max . . ." Mrs. Hunter opened the front door and threw her arms around his shoulders. "You were his best friend. . . . What did we do so wrong that both our sons would . . . would want to . . ."

Silence.

"Stay right there." Mrs. Hunter went back into the house and returned with Brett's skateboard, guitar and compact disc booklet. "His clothes are probably too big for you, but if you want any of this, it's yours. Throwing it all out or garage selling it would just be so shameful."

"Thank you, I'll . . . I'll have to learn to play guitar now, but thank you."

"He loved those records. I always thought it was the most horrible noise, but it was something else for him."

"You didn't do anything wrong, Mrs. Hunter. Trust me, it's the worst thing in the world when you start blaming yourself for other people's decisions."

"Thank you for coming, Max." Mrs. Hunter closed the front door. "We need to be alone now."

He sat on the lawn and unzipped the two hundred-capacity CD booklet. The first four entries were *Abbey Road, Let It Be* and the double-disc *White Album.*

"No damn way." Max laughed and flipped to find *A Hard Day's Night, Rubber Soul, Imagine, Band on the Run* and *All Things Must Pass.* "He was lying about the Beatles being the Faggles all along? He actually had *all the albums?* All the *solo albums?"*

He sat there laughing for a long time, then carried everything back to his apartment and finally walked to Kapkovian Pacific.

"—sold it all on the fuckin' 'Net—"

"—didn't even know he still went to—"

"—hear about that runner kid who—"

"—thought that happened last year—"

"—last year was his fucking *broth*—"

"—hear about Ian's bro last weekend at—"

"—down on a girl for the first time—"

"—so damn great, a bitch is actually—"

"—fucking your face, I know, I know—"

"—acquired taste, that's for fuckin' sure—"

Max ignored the gossip and headed straight for the classroom at the end of the hallway.

"Oh . . . Max, you're here." Ms. Lovelace sat behind her desk. "You must feel terrible right now. I'm so sorry about Brett."

"Why did you do it, Ms. Lovelace? In that hotel room?"

"What . . . what hotel room? What are you talking about, Max?"

"Everybody knows. You did something teachers should never do."

She forced a weak smile.

"If you ever need anyone to talk to, Max, I'm available." Ms. Lovelace withdrew a ballpoint pen and a Post-It note from her desk. "This is my home number. Don't hesitate to call if you ever need to talk to *anyone*. Self-destruction spreads like a virus, and I will never lose a single student to it again as long as I live."

"You really shouldn't worry . . ." Max took the Post-It note. "I'll be okay, Miss Lovelace."

He walked back into the hallway. Thousands of students rushed to class, all buzzing with hearsay about Trevor, Quinn, Brett, Ashley and the countless camera crews outside beyond the parking lot.

"Hey there." Max placed a hand gently on Julia's shoulder. "How are you holding up?"

"Oh God, Max." She stood with her forehead pressed against her locker, crying into the cold gray steel. "The custody lawyers called last night. That's what I was going to tell Brett when I went over to his house. The judge decided not to review my emancipation forms because I got a detention yesterday, so I have to go back to Anchorage tonight and live with some foster family I've never met before. God, I can't even *see* my mom and dad until I turn *eighteen*."

"You're *leaving*? You mean you're leaving *tonight* and you're not coming *back?*"

"We'll see each other again, Max. We can still talk on the phone and write letters and remember how special prom was and still be friends even though we'll be in two different cities."

"No, no, no, no, no," Max cried, shaking his head. "You can't *leave. * Not *now.*"

"Don't be sad, Max." She held his hands in hers and smeared her tears across his cheeks. "Oh God, I just wish it were yesterday again for one minute. I just wish it were yesterday again so, so, so much, because yesterday the world was still good."

Max tried to smile.

THE END

↗ S.L.U.T. STATS

53%:

Percentage of failed American marriages in the 1990s
[Source: The U.S. Bureau of the Census]

28%:

Percentage of married men who have committed adultery

17%:

Of married women
[Source: *USA Today*, December 21, 1998]

23%:

Percentage of married Americans who believe "infidelity is an unavoidable part of married life today"
[Source: *Time* magazine, August 31, 1998]

ASHLEY O., 19

WASHINGTON, D.C.

"I don't understand why anyone would want to fall in love when you see people in relationships get heartbroken all the time. Like, is it really any better to date someone for eight months and then have to break up with them than to just meet them at a party and then have sex with them?"

"Stamford, CT—The 9-year-old boy who was arrested on charges of raping a 7-year-old girl in the bathroom at Roxbury Elementary School has been removed from the school, officials said yesterday. . . . The boy was arrested Tuesday in the sexual assault, which allegedly occurred in late March. Police are not saying what charges were filed against the youth."

—THE STAMFORD ADVOCATE, APRIL 17, 2003

"Denver, CO—Police said a group of fifth graders tried to poison a schoolmate by putting pills, glue, lead and chalk in her drinks. . . . Police learned of the case Tuesday after the eleven-year-old complained to teachers that she had found the items in her water bottle and soda over three days. . . . 'They said that they didn't like her and that they wanted to hurt her,' school principal Sally Edwards said Thursday."

—THE ASSOCIATED PRESS, JANUARY 17, 2003

"Philadelphia, Pennsylvania (AP)—A 16-year-old boy was lured by his new girlfriend into a field where three of his friends robbed and bludgeoned him, police said, in a beating investigators called one of the most vicious they had ever seen. Jason Sweeney was killed as the result of a scheme the girl and three boys concocted to rob Sweeney of $500 in cash to buy drugs, police Sgt. Kathleen McGowan said. Justina Morley, 15, and the boys—Edward Batzig Jr., 16; Nicholas Coia, 16; and his brother Dominic Coia, 17—were charged as adults with murder and related offenses. The boys had grown up together, police said. Sweeney's mother said her son seemed happy with his girlfriend of two weeks. 'He thought she was a nice girl,' Dawn Sweeney said. 'He wanted me to meet her.'"

—THE ASSOCIATED PRESS, JUNE 6, 2003

"Philadelphia, Pennsylvania—The four teens—after a group hug—then robbed the victim, dividing up the $500 that Sweeney had earned at his construction job and went on a drug binge, police said. 'We took Sweeney's wallet and split up the money, and we partied beyond redemption,' Dominic Coia, 18, told detectives, according to a transcript of his June 3 police interview."

—THE ASSOCIATED PRESS, JUNE 19, 2003

↗ S.L.U.T. STATS

47,000,000+:

Americans aged ten to nineteen years

19,000,000:

Americans aged twenty to twenty-four years

21%:

Percentage of the U.S. population aged ten to twenty-four years ("Generation Y")
[Source: U.S. Bureau of the Census]

ADDENDUM

Turning Twenty in the Year of the Damned:
Assorted Reflections on My World, My Generation, My Penis

AUTHOR'S NOTE (2/7/03):

In the two weeks since completing this memoir, the Author has frequented the gym on a daily basis—working up his Stamina and Endurance—desperately attempting to bring himself back to his mid-adolescent Vigor. Subsequently, the Author is thrilled to reveal that His Penis is functional once again, much to the Delight of his Beautiful Girlfriend and the World at large. Thank you for your concern.

↗ *January 23, 2003*

10:35 p.m.

The Dark Hour of Twelve now approaches, My Countrymen: Soon I shall forever graduate from my Damned Teenage Years, abandoning eternally my Adolescence and experiencing Manhood for the first time upon this Rotten Planet Earth.

And yet, I am sad inside. What explains this incorrigible Misery? What causes this endless Melancholy? Gods! Answer me! O, that this too, too sullied flesh would melt, Thaw, and resolve itself into a Dew![1]

For the Sake of King Jesus in Heaven, my having survived twenty whole years without serious injury or contraction of any venereal diseases should be an occasion marked by Hope, Joy and Naked Drunken Harlots Sitting On My Face and Wiggling Around Like Dying Fish or Something. After all, two centuries ago, the average human life span was less than thirty years, according to *Rising Life Expectancy: A Global History* (Cambridge University Press, 2001).

But instead of Revelry at my continued Vitality and Vigor, my conscience is racked with the unmistakable sensation that something is Amiss and Wrong. The origin of this perverted suffering eludes all my self-analytical resources, but I have a pretty good idea that it has something to do with the fact My Penis isn't working and Oh God, My Goddamn Penis isn't working, Oh Christ, Oh God, Oh Lord, Oh Jesus, Oh Fuck! Fuck! Fuck! Fuck! NOOOOOOOOOOOOOOOOOOOOOO!!!

---

1 / The Author has no qualms about quoting lesser writers without attribution. Especially when they've been dead for 400 years.

11:02 p.m.

Now don't go thinking I'm Impotent at Age Nineteen or anything silly like that, you silly little silly-sillies. My Penis has a long history (so to speak) of functioning smoothly to the satisfaction of both its proprietor and primary care giver(s). However, the last few weeks have proven unsettling: You see, during a recent lovemaking session with My Beautiful Girlfriend, My Penis failed to make it past the Dreaded Two-Minute Mark.

Now, I realize it takes a big man (so to speak) to publicly admit he's having such difficulties with his Flesh Flute. However, Untruth is a Sin beyond my journalistic capacities: I am a fledgling creature of Honesty. And so it is with utter Shame and Regret that I admit this shortcoming (so to speak) of my historically trustworthy genitals. Especially in this Age of Female Orgasms.

And the worst I've yet to admit: Ever since that horrible morning when My Penis failed me, I've been unable to maintain an erection for Fear of failing once again. (HolyShitHolyShitHolyGodMyLifeIsOverOhGodNoNoNo!) It's circular psychosexual logic: Constantly worrying about keeping it up with My Beautiful Girlfriend is what's been keeping me from performing to the best of my abilities, but I can't stop worrying because I've already proven myself to be a Thirty-Second Wonder.

"Are you sure you're not the least bit gay?" My Beautiful Girlfriend asked last weekend after another failed night of Attempted Love. "I mean, just the least little bit gay? You know, just like the least little bit?"

Which is not exactly the kind of thing a Straight Man in his Sexual Prime wants to hear whilst battling such wretched Impotence. But Alas, this all happened once before—two years ago—on the night I should've lost mine own Innocence, mine own Virginity, mine own Virtue in the Eyes of Mine Lord Christ.

Three days had passed since my High School Graduation: I lay naked in my childhood bed, my girlfriend at the time equally Naked beside me upon the mattress. I knew my First Time was destined to transpire that night, but I had no idea how to propose the carnal consideration. I mean, Good Lord, how do you ask something like that from such a wholesome, upstanding young woman?

"So are you going to fuck me now or what?" she asked, suckling my manhood.

"Okay!" I said, already reaching for the Trojan condom under my bed. "Yay!"

Of course, I felt simultaneously excited and terrified at the prospect of Losing my Virginity. This was something I'd fantasized about thousands of nights before, stroking myself in the Dark, dreaming of days to come (so to speak). Unfortunately, something was missing from the night's proceedings. And you guessed it: That something was My Penis.

"Um . . . Just give me a minute," I pleaded, furiously stroking myself in Sheer Panic, praying to Mine Lord Christ for One More Erection. "I just need some time to . . . oh God . . . Work, you rotten son of a bitch."

"Maybe you should drive me home now?" she asked forty-five minutes later, as I lay my head upon her chest, sobbing like a little girl who had lost her fucking teddy bear.

11:59 p.m.

Goodbye, Sweet Teenage World
Goodbye—

"Washington, D.C.—American citizens working for al-Qaeda overseas can legally be targeted and killed by the CIA under President Bush's rules for the war on terrorism, U.S. officials say. The authority to kill U.S. citizens is granted under a secret finding signed by the president after the Sept. 11 attacks that directs the CIA to covertly attack al-Qaeda anywhere in the world."
—THE ASSOCIATED PRESS, DEC. 4, 2002

Make No Mistake: The Human Race is going straight to Hell and there is no turning back. Mankind has fucked-up one too many times to be allowed to exist anymore. We have entered the War to End All Wars, and the Days of Man are drawing to an Apocalyptic Close:

"Jabaliya Refugee Camp, Gaza Strip—The militant group Hamas, which has carried out scores of suicide bombings in Israel, urged Iraq on Friday to copy its tactics and send thousands of attackers with explosives strapped to their bodies into a battle against the West."
—THE ASSOCIATED PRESS, JAN. 10, 2003

So here come the Suicide Soldiers from the Land of Allah. Well, fuck it: My generation never held any hope for the Future anyway, so why even bother continuing the Human Race?

"A teenage 'chugging contest' in an upscale home near Burr Ridge turned into rape when a 16-year-old girl passed out and four young men performed sex acts on her—and scrawled offensive words on her body with a marker—while they videotaped their crimes, a Cook County prosecutor said Friday," wrote the *Chicago Sun-Times* January 11, 2003. The *Sun-Times* later elucidated:

"At some point [around 2:30 a.m.], the girl went into a bedroom and vomited, and the video was made shortly after, authorities say. In court records and statements at earlier hearings, prosecutors said [18-year-old Sonny] Smith maneuvered the camera and coached the participants. They accuse [17-year-old Adrian] Missbrenner and [17-year-old Burim] Bezeri of sexually assaulting the girl. They say [18-year-old Christopher] Robbins forced oral sex on her, [18-year-old Jason] Thomas wrote on her leg with a

black marker and [18-year-old Joshua] Kott spit on the girl and
drew on her."

Indeed. Today's teenage populace is comprised of heartless fucking Animals, and I'm
glad to no longer share any part of it. For the Love of God, 25 percent of American adolescents believe it's acceptable to physically force intercourse on a girl if she's intoxicated, according to *The Journal of School Health*.[2]

And that number goes up to 62 percent if the girl is dressed "provocatively."

"This one girl in my class gave me a note that said she wanted
to have sex with someone and she wanted it to be me, but then my
mom found it in my back pocket when she was doing the laundry. I
guess she was pretty pissed off, because the girl's only like
twelve or whatever, and I guess my mom thinks that's weird or
something."
—BILLY G., 13, PHILADELPHIA, PENNSYLVANIA

"A few months ago my boyfriend wanted me to have sex with him and
his best friend at the same time. I didn't really want to, but he
said he'd break up with me if I didn't, so we tried it out. It
was kind of weird at first, but after a while it was okay, I
guess. He broke up with me a month later anyway."
—MELANIE M., 18, GREENSBORO, NORTH CAROLINA

Of course, I'm not a Saint by any means. No, I'm just your everyday (formerly) teenage
male: Curious, Covetous, Lustful and Weak. As such, I've engaged in more than a few
of these meaningless weekend hook-ups: Titillating, inconsequential Petting Sessions
serving no other purpose than Instant Gratification and a fairly convenient place to
deposit a few teaspoons of Excess Teenage Semen. As American Adolescents, promis-

2 / Republished in Sexual Teens, Sexual Media: Investigating Media's Influence on
Adolescent Sexuality, Lawrence Erlbaum Associates, 2002.

cuity is not only expected of us but *respected* as well—in nearly every perceivable social circle, at every booze-replete Saturday night party.

"Sex is the only form of human behavior viewed as uncontrollable in teenagers," writes nationally syndicated columnist Cal Thomas in a June 8, 2001 essay.

And yet, astonishingly, 53 percent of teenage girls and 41 percent of boys staunchly believe sex before marriage is "always wrong," according to a major 1998 *New York Times*/CBS News census of American high school students. In addition, teenage girls are three times more likely to attempt suicide if they're sexually active—according to a recent national survey quoted in *USA Today*—and teenage boys are *six* times more likely. What in the Holy Fuck is going *on* here?

Let's start at the beginning. The Sexual Revolution of the 1960s is generally viewed as a positive development in the American social fabric: It is grouped with the civil rights, antiwar and feminist movements,[3] and only religious extremists now argue that unrestrained pleasure-seeking is detrimental to the wellbeing of society. As rightwing author Suzanne Labin wrote in her paranoid *Hippies, Drugs and Promiscuity* (Arlington House, 1970):

"One obvious consequence of the hippie philosophy—that is, the primacy of personal pleasure over any other value—is the claim for total liberty of sexual experiences, including the right to change partners when the mood hits. . . . Oh, my happy and sad friends along the hashish trail, I fear not only for our civilization, but also for you. . . . You have no emotional ties to each other, when you should have taught us love."

The 1950s and '60s were two very different eras for American teenagers, partly thanks to the Vietnam War and partly thanks to the Food and Drug Administration's 1960 approval of an inexpensive pill that rendered the female body incapable of pregnancy. The combination of widespread youth resentment toward nearly all mainstream

3 / Feminism: Philosophy popularized in the late 1960s. Asserts that women—all victims of a nonexistent "patriarchy"—no longer belong to men in sexual relationships. Likewise, men no longer belong to women, thus antiquating monogamy, marriage, commitment and human affection. [See: Valerie Solanas, "The S.C.U.M. [Society for Cutting Up Men] Manifesto," 1968]

(pro-Christian/pro-Vietnam) values and the immediately ubiquitous Pill caused the number of sexually active teenagers to skyrocket from 23 percent before 1960 to 42 percent in 1968 and 55 percent in 1972. In effect, millions upon millions of young Americans discarded the social convention held most dear since their nation's infancy, choosing instead a new generation-wide maxim: Cure Virginity Now.

"There is a certain kind of girl who enjoys men but is awkward waking up beside a stranger," divulges a personal ad in the December 7, 1967 *Berkeley Barb*—at one time a widely read youth newspaper—adding, "Good looking, discreet, adaptable young man will perform and disappear. If you are pretty, call."

Hundreds of similar daily notices filled underground hippie weeklies across the nation, making it easier than ever for sexually curious boys and girls to find willing overnight partners in big cities and small towns alike. But what, it must be asked, was the actual *meaning* of our parents' Sexual Revolution? What was the *reason* for it?

"A West Virginia University journalist, reporting on sex as a fact of life on campus, found students agreeing on reasons for premarital intercourse," wrote *Look* magazine in 1967. "The reasons: physical desire; to show adults you are going to do exactly what you want to do regardless of what they think; to release tension."

Sexual attraction? Check.

Youthful rebellion? Check.

Stress relief? Check.

Free *Love*? Naaah. In fact, meaningless, uncommitted intercourse was the Sexual Revolution's only real objective or outcome—and maybe this is why more than half of all Baby Boomers have been divorced at least once, according to the U.S. Census Bureau.

"The uneasy bedfellowship of the sexual revolution and feminism produced an odd tension in which all the moral restraints governing nature disappeared, but so did nature," writes University of Chicago professor Allan Bloom in his controversial bestseller *The Closing of the American Mind* (Simon & Schuster, 1987). "The exhilaration of liberation has evaporated, however, for it is unclear what exactly was liberated. . . . [Adolescents] are not sure what they feel for one another and are without guidance about what to do with whatever they may feel. . . . There are some men and women at the age of sixteen who have nothing more to learn about the erotic."

And that was seventeen years ago.

"Aging research provides a good example of the way in which biomedical science in recent years has become an international venture moving back and forth across national boundaries. If the problems of human aging are solved by one or more of today's research approaches, the ultimate solution cannot be fairly claimed by any nation or any particular laboratory or group of laboratories."
—THE FRAGILE SPECIES BY LEWIS THOMAS, M.D.

Number of American men taking the anti-impotence drug Viagra: **9,000,000**
[Source: Pfizer, Inc.]

Two years ago

"So are you going to kiss me or just sit there?" the Girl asks.

I'm comfortably occupying the front seat of my Awesome 1984 Dodge MiniVan. She's in the seat beside me, wearing a skintight pink shirt that shows vastly more than it hides. We're parked in the driveway in front of her house. The engine is turned off and I can't help but feel excruciatingly awkward. Our first date has gone pretty well, judging from the sound of things. But Jesus, I just *met* this girl. Do I really want to throw myself into another one of these meaningless carnal escapades?

"I don't know," I say. "Should we?"

Yeah, I sound like a real fuckin' Romeo.

"Oh . . ." She pouts. "You don't *like* me?"

"No, I like you a lot. It's just . . . I'm sorry, my girlfriend broke up with me last week and it just seems too soon to be doing this, you know?"

Silence.

"It was really the first relationship I've ever been in," I confide. "I guess it would be a little weird, going from that end of the spectrum to . . . I mean, you're *nice* and all—don't get me wrong—but obviously we don't share some kind of deep emotional longing or anything."

"Well, it was nice meeting you." She smiles and unbuckles her seatbelt. "Call me, we'll hang out again sometime. Unless you want to come inside, but I guess you wouldn't."

MEMO FROM BRAIN TO PENIS: Hey Penis, let's not go inside!
MEMO FROM PENIS TO BRAIN [Re: "Bad Idea"]: Ha! Ha! That's a good one, old buddy!

"Sure!" I joyously shriek. "Why not?"

We stroll up the walkway to her front door, which she unlocks quietly, holding her index finger to her lips and alerting me that I shouldn't make much noise. After all, we wouldn't want to wake Mommy and Daddy, would we? No, we wouldn't. Goddamn, something about the possibility of getting caught just sends a warm shiver down my testicles. Not yet, Penis. But soon. Very, very soon.

The door creaks open. The house is dark and her parents are fast asleep. My heart is pounding and adrenaline is coursing through my veins like black tar heroin. The girl leads me down the stairs into her small bedroom, tiptoeing all the way. We lock hands and our bodies commit to each other in Luscious Teenage Passion: Her lips come closer as we fall onto the soft bed. Yes, Penis, your time has come! *Rise*, Penis! *Rise*, I say! *Rise*, damn you! *Rise!*

MEMO FROM BRAIN TO PENIS: For God's sake, Penis, don't you remember the beautiful relationship we've been in for the last three months? Haven't you realized that Love is more fulfilling than Lust in every way that matters? Goddammit, Penis! Tonight's Squirm-Session won't make a single difference to you tomorrow, but if you don't give in—if you prove just once that you're more than a slave to your own hormonal impulses—wouldn't that be the true victory? The true "score," as it were?

MEMO FROM PENIS TO BRAIN: Whatever, dude.

"Wait," I say, still holding the girl in my arms. "Wouldn't this mean more to you if we actually *cared* about each other a little bit? Don't you *want* something deeper than this?"

(Long, awkward silence.)

"You make me so wet," she explains, wiggling her tongue around the insides of my ears for the next ten minutes.

MEMO FROM PENIS TO BRAIN: Nice try. Sucker.

"Sex feels good. You may be aware of this fact already . . . By the same token, having sex with a prostitute is degrading and can actually feel bad. Ask anyone who has tried it. Cheap sex and one-night-stands and sex on the first date all tend to fall into that same category. It often feels bad. . . . It is a cheap thrill that has little or no value."

—THE TEENAGER'S GUIDE TO THE REAL WORLD BY MARSHALL BRIAN

"Sex without love is an empty experience. But as empty experiences go, it's one of the best."

—WOODY ALLEN

The Death of Young Love is Complete, my friends. Of course, love can flourish in sexual relationships—I'm not suggesting that true love means celibacy, as I personally enjoy spitting (or ejaculating) in God's face whenever My Penis decides to follow orders—but America has become the Land of the Free-Time.

Incidentally, the Centers for Disease Control and Prevention estimate that 50 percent of fourteen- and fifteen-year-olds get drunk at least once a month, not to mention 79 percent of eighteen-year-olds—*the very same numbers as those sexually active in each age group.* The Sexual Revolution of the 1960s paved the way for the Hook-Up Culture, and Generation X personified it,[4] but this inseparable juxtaposition of physical intimacy and intoxication starting in *prepubescent children* is something new and ultimately terrifying.

Which brings us to the simple, single reason a majority of American teenagers believe premarital sex is morally unrespectable even though four out of five partake in the act: *We're trying to fuck our way out of Fear.* Morality is irrelevant. When individuality is crushed and humanity might very well annihilate itself at any moment, why *not* seek out fleeting pleasures at every opportunity? It doesn't *hurt* anyone, right?

You can go to War and Die for your country at eighteen, but take a sip of beer prior to twenty-one—or have sex prior to eighteen in most states—and you're an Outlaw. Meanwhile, a significant portion of those *over* twenty-one diet religiously, inject themselves with "age-reducing" chemicals/hormones (6.2 million adults had cosmetic operations in 2002, 40 percent more than in 1997),[5] and dress in the trendiest brand names, all in order to look like teenagers again. Our culture worships Youth, and punishes the Young as Savages.

(No wonder the young are savages.)

"UNITED NATIONS—North Korea has told the U.N. it would consider it an act of war if the Security Council imposes sanctions over the continuing nuclear weapons program dispute . . . Washington's top arms control diplomat said Wednesday that it is time to refer the matter to the United Nations Security Council, which in turn could hit Pyongyang with sanctions."
—CNN, JANUARY 22, 2003

---

4 / The difference between Generation X and Generation V: While Gen. X-ers are frustrated and snooty because they have nothing meaningful in their lives (and no meaningful heroes), Gen. V celebrates this meaninglessness wholeheartedly.
5 / American Academy of Facial Plastic and Reconstructive Surgery, 2003.

"I definitely feel fearful of relationships even though my parents
are still together. Any time I actually pair emotion with hooking
up I get hurt, so I'm always telling myself to be 'more of a guy'
about physical intimacy. . . . I've definitely saved myself a lot
of pain by detaching myself from physical intimacy, and I'm a lot
more sexually satisfied. I'm probably coming off like a cold-
hearted bitch right now but I figure guys do it so I can too."
—MIA S., 19, YALE UNIVERSITY

I'll concede there might be some infinitesimal spark of Hope somewhere in the World—
most likely in the void between the fringe that cares and the mainstream that can be
persuaded to care—but this Hope will need to vanquish some seriously Dark Fear in
order to prevail. People across the nation are Afraid of the Future and Afraid of each
other. We're Afraid to Connect, Afraid to Commit, Afraid of Compassion.

So forget Love, everybody. Why not just get it over with and Fuck like wild animals
today? Why strive for anything substantive in our lives when Nuclear Armageddon is
right around the corner and the name of the game is Instant Gratification?

Well, don't ask me, Dear Countrymen.

My Fucking Dick doesn't even work.

Marty Beckerman is the twenty-year-old Spokesman for His Generation, raised in tropical Anchorage, Alaska, and currently living in Washington, D.C. His occasionally controversial writing has appeared in *The Anchorage Daily News, New York Press, Disinformation, Get Underground, Ain't It Cool News,* and *Penthouse Online.* At age seventeen Beckerman self-published his first book— *Death to All Cheerleaders: One Adolescent Journalist's Cheerful Diatribe Against Teenage Plasticity*—which has since developed a worldwide cult following of embittered outcasts. He is currently studying media psychology and literature at American University. His favorite sexual position is 69.

Visit his website at www.martybeckerman.com.